ALSO BY GEOF KAUFMAN

Mastering Your Choices (Nonfiction)
The Rainbow Solution (Screenplay)

A Human...

GEOF KAUFMAN

BALBOA.
PRESS

A DIVISION OF HAY HOUSE

Balboa Press books may be ordered through booksellers or by contacting:

Balboa Press
A Division of Hay House
1663 Liberty Drive
Bloomington, IN 47403
www.balboapress.com
1 (877) 407-4847

Because of the dynamic nature of the Internet, any web addresses or links contained in this book may have changed since publication and may no longer be valid. The views expressed in this work are solely those of the author and do not necessarily reflect the views of the publisher, and the publisher hereby disclaims any responsibility for them.

The author of this book does not dispense medical advice or prescribe the use of any technique as a form of treatment for physical, emotional, or medical problems without the advice of a physician, either directly or indirectly. The intent of the author is only to offer information of a general nature to help you in your quest for emotional and spiritual well-being. In the event you use any of the information in this book for yourself, which is your constitutional right, the author and the publisher assume no responsibility for your actions.

Any people depicted in stock imagery provided by Thinkstock are models, and such images are being used for illustrative purposes only.
Certain stock imagery © Thinkstock.

Print information available on the last page.

ISBN: 978-1-5043-6658-8 (sc)
ISBN: 978-1-5043-6660-1 (hc)
ISBN: 978-1-5043-6659-5 (e)

Library of Congress Control Number: 2016915589

Balboa Press rev. date: 11/01/2016

DEDICATION

I DEDICATE this book to the timeless and infinite energy in the universe that sometimes takes tangible form, including that of human beings, and to the spiritual awakening that is now happening to evolve our species. In short, I dedicate it to us all.

Acknowledgment

Various people, places, events, books, movies, and other inspirational experiences over the course of my first fifty years have culminated in my current life perspectives and the ideas offered in this book. Having said that, I would like to express my heartfelt appreciation to and acknowledge the creative consultation and editing assistance provided to me during the creation of this book by loved ones Erika Villegas, Sarah Kaufman, Carolyn Kaufman, and Dorothy Hemenway. I love and thank you.

PREFACE

THIS book is my take on the evolution of human beings, but it is not about mutant genes, scientific experimentation, or super powers. It is about beginning to understand the unlimited relationship between the capabilities of the mind and the awareness of the soul. This evolution is evident as I continue to encounter more and more people who have begun to recognize the importance of choosing to be happy now instead of choosing the stressful have-to-do's we were taught.

I have no doubt that the ideas I write about in the following pages will speak to the awakening consciousness of you who are meant to receive them.

PROLOGUE

XANDER watched the lines in the man's face soften and his body relax as the pain gradually dissolved. One by one, Xander became aware of his own senses again. He could hear the man's breathing deepen, becoming audible despite the murmuring of the crowd that had formed around them. Feeling the balance restored to the energy and heartbeat beneath his hands, he sensed a mix of energies surrounding him and settled back to look up to meet the eyes of the curious people who had gathered to watch. He sensed and saw confusion, skepticism, relief, awe, and disbelief. Even though he could only imagine the thoughts of the spectators, he had learned through experience he was often right. Of course, the thoughts were not anything unusual. They would be the typical ones. *What just happened? Oh my God! I don't believe it!* Then he heard actual voices.

"Holy shit!" was exclaimed by a young man who looked like he could still be in high school. "Did you just save his life?"

A woman who looked to be in her early twenties took a step forward and asked excitedly, "What did you do?"

The questions paused as the crowd awaited a response to satisfy their individual, internal questions, and in most cases, he knew, to judge him.

Xander tried to think of what he actually did. He remembered he was on one of his carefree walks on the campus of the local college. He didn't attend classes there, but the school was close to his apartment and was beautifully landscaped. It was a meditative practice he had, to walk the paths in just about any kind of park-like setting and observe the environment through each of his senses. He remembered feeling the warmth of the sun each time the cool breeze stopped. He heard people, birds, and the traffic, and he listened to the concert of raking, weed-eating, and a distant lawnmower. There were people everywhere, sitting and playing on the grass, jogging and riding bikes, and walking. He remembered watching a couple walking toward him on the sidewalk. He thought they looked about his age—twenty or so. Their individual auras were moving smoothly and easily blended into a harmonious cloud of energy surrounding them. The man's energy had a tan tint to it and felt a little off to Xander, but there was nothing specific he could identify. The couple's love for each other was clear, and Xander noticed they weren't speaking, simply smiling, holding hands, and enjoying each other as they walked. He looked away and smiled himself, also enjoying their combined, positive contribution to the world in the moment as they passed him. A few steps later, he felt an internal nudge and glanced back at them. They had stopped, and the woman had turned to the man, who was off balance and wobbling. Xander could see that the man's energy had changed. What was tan had turned to a dark brown, swirling mass that looked like a swamp or thick, disgusting soup. The man's knees buckled and his body crumpled sideways. Luckily for him, he fell so his head and face hit the grass instead of the concrete.

Xander didn't remember making a conscious choice about it, but he found himself quickly moving toward the couple even before the woman started screaming. He didn't remember thinking about what he was doing as he knelt beside the man and rolled him over onto his back. Above where the man's heart should be, Xander could see the eye of the storm in the dark brown swirling soup that was the man's energy cloud. Xander did remember experiencing déjà vu, as he had seen this type of energy before. This type… and worse. It was never good. He placed one of his hands lightly on the man's chest, and the other on the grass. He began visualizing a surge of energy, pure white, coming down from the sky and through his own body into the ground. Then he envisioned healing energy, a light green light, coming up from the earth through his hand, up his arm and across his chest, and down through his other arm into the man. He pictured the green energy saturating the man's chest and mixing with the brown energy that was surrounding his heart.

A few more spectators joined the others at the scene. Xander's attention returned to the present when one of them exclaimed, "That's not how you do CPR!"

Xander ignored the comment and maintained his focus. He saw the healing energy he had introduced start to dilute and slow the swirling brown energy. After a minute or so, the brown swamp disappeared.

This guy's lucky, Xander thought. *That doesn't always work.*

He made eye contact with the woman who had asked the question a moment ago.

"I just helped him balance his energy."

The woman companion was sobbing and hugging the man, who had opened his eyes but was obviously disoriented. Without breaking her hug, she turned her head toward Xander and mouthed *thank you*.

He nodded to her and stood up, feeling various spikes of energy, which he had come to understand are associated with sadness, relief, bewilderment, and anger.

That's okay. People feel, he thought.

Xander chose not to linger in that moment now that it had passed and, ignoring the various comments and the approaching sirens, he walked on with a continued appreciation for the world around him.

CHAPTER 1

THERE was nothing special about the birth itself, or even the pregnancy. Almost ten months to the alleged day of conception, Tracy Noxx endured what she believed was a fairly typical labor experience. She had attended all of her routine medical appointments, and so this appeared to her to be a normal experience, although she didn't have any personal history with which to compare it. There was some pain, some discomfort, and a huge relief immediately after delivery. The hospital and staff weren't special, and nothing in the delivery room stood out as extraordinary. Aside from the doctor and nurses, Rebecca, Tracy's older sister by three years, was the only other person in the room. The partner in the conception had disappeared seven months ago, but Tracy was only mildly surprised. They may have been in love, but it was not the kind or amount of love that lasted under these circumstances. In truth, she was a little relieved. She knew all too well what could happen when a mother and father don't agree on how to raise a child. She and Rebecca had lived through that experience, and Tracy, for one, wouldn't wish it upon anyone. It was obvious that she and the baby's father would have embraced different parenting styles, especially since he had made it clear that being in his child's life wasn't his responsibility… or even a priority of any kind.

Rebecca did her part. She did her best to motivate Tracy, acting more like an athletic coach than a cheerleader, shouting lots of canned, motivational phrases like, "Come on! You can do it!" and "Push through the pain! You're almost there!" With Tracy's final push and her last yell, the baby was born. An ultrasound some time ago had revealed the sex, so all involved knew it was a boy. Tracy was exhausted in all ways, especially emotionally, but all thoughts stopped when she realized her baby wasn't crying.

She squeezed Rebecca's hand even harder and tilted her head up to look. "What's wrong? Why isn't he crying?"

The doctor still held the baby while the nurse cleared his throat and nose. Still no crying. The doctor and nurse were both just looking down at the baby.

Tracy yelled, "What's wrong with my baby?"

The doctor handed the baby to the nurse, lifted his head to look at Tracy and pulled his mask down to reveal a broad smile.

"Nothing whatsoever. He is perfectly healthy and beautiful. Congratulations, Mom."

Rebecca was as confused as Tracy, and she asked the obvious question. "But why isn't he crying?"

The doctor glanced over in the direction of the baby, who was being cleaned, weighed, and measured by the nurse.

"Most babies do cry, since that's how they communicate. They usually experience the moment of birth as one of the most traumatic culture shocks of their lives. It's unusual, but once in a while, a baby, like yours, just doesn't seem to feel the need to cry. Just like adults, some babies just naturally handle stress better than others."

The nurse finished swaddling the infant, walked to the bed, and handed him to Tracy.

"You see?" she said to Tracy.

Tracy finally released Rebecca's hand to take the baby, joining her sister in a chorus of soprano-pitched exclamations, "Awww."

The nurse said, "I've never actually seen a newborn looking this… at peace."

Tracy looked in wonderment at her new son. It was true. He seemed to be perfectly at ease.

"Does he have a name yet?" asked the nurse.

Tracy was crying but smiling.

"I named him long ago. Xander. I wanted him to have a strong-sounding name. I want him to be confident and true to himself."

"Well, it seems to fit," the doctor said. "He certainly doesn't seem worried about anything. Happy birthday, Xander."

CHAPTER 2

F OR the first few years, Xander lived an ordinary, uneventful life with his mother. Tracy had lived alone ever since her boyfriend, Xander's father by conception only, had taken the path of least resistance, at least for himself. The only aspect of Xander's life that was even remotely different was that he was healthier than the average baby. Along the way, Tracy had made some conscious and, at times, unorthodox choices for her baby's health. They seemed to have paid off. She even found a job as a virtual executive assistant that allowed her to work from anywhere, provided she had her laptop and access to Wi-Fi. Sometimes, however, despite what looked like positive outcomes, her choices came with negative side effects, normally in the form of criticism from other members of society, including medical professionals, educational professionals, and even her own sister.

One such choice was based on her sincere belief that society made a lot of decisions based on fear. She believed fear controlled people, and so it had the power to influence peoples' decisions. More importantly, fear gave those in power the means to increase profits. Tracy thought a prime example of that control was the practice of vaccinating. Despite any of her researched arguments against unnaturally injecting her healthy baby, fear of what could happen backed up the opposing arguments for just about every adult she knew. Of course, Tracy also believed that people tended to support what they had experienced, whether or not it was a good experience.

For some reason, Xander's remarkable health didn't seem to change others' opinions, but Tracy didn't care. At least, she cared more that

Xander was happy and healthy than about the opinions of others. And so, Tracy had taken Xander to all of the scheduled well-baby appointments but had declined the shots. Everyone she knew agreed that Xander was as healthy as could be. So whenever she had the doctors and nurses in her face telling her why she needed to vaccinate her baby, she would remind them that her baby was perfectly healthy by their own standards. She assured them she would deal with any health problems that might arise. Whether Tracy was right or it was just luck, Xander remained healthy.

Despite Tracy's consistent fight over vaccinations with those whom, including Rebecca, she referred to as *damn dominoes* (since they fall whichever way they're pushed), Tracy was very comfortable with her choices. Xander's health continued to provide her with validation. Also, Xander gave all signs that he was happy… or at least, not unhappy. He was very alert, moving his eyes and head to any sound or changes in light, and his body was active, with his eyes and limbs always moving, as if he were warming up for an athletic event. There were a few odd things about him, but they were not negative things. Xander rarely cried, but even stranger was the fact that his face hardly ever changed expression. Although it's common for babies to seem like they're practicing making funny faces for the amusement of others, flapping their eyebrows or flexing their upper lips into accidental snarls, Xander performed none of those personal exercises. Unless he was crying on some unusual occasion, he looked as though he was merely observing. Tracy thought he looked peaceful, and she was content with him being at peace.

CHAPTER 3

ASIDE from noting his lack of crying and changing facial expressions, nobody, including Xander, realized anything was different about him until he was four years old. He was in preschool and sitting on the floor along with the other children, but even in the group, it was as if he were alone. He did not dislike people; it was just that he didn't think they were any more special than anything else around him. He saw them as moving objects. He didn't see people as uninteresting. He simply thought the rest of the world was equally as interesting as people. The mat on which he sat, the blocks he stacked, the hum of the air conditioning—everything held its own interest to him. He piled up blocks randomly, unevenly, and imagined connectors joining them, supporting them. He saw the colored borders and letters painted on the sides, but he naturally saw other things as well. He would sometimes place a new block on top of another, offset it, and then slowly twist it to watch the formation change. Everything around him fascinated him.

His different behavior led some people to believe there was something not quite right with him. Some of the more ignorant and opinionated adults thought him autistic. Those same people did not think he had what they considered the glamorous kind of autism that affected some of our famous, historical geniuses, but the kind that causes fear and negatively labels so many people as "weird."

A spider crawled from a nearby corner and inched its way up the hem of Xander's shorts. He watched it and marveled at its uniqueness. He imagined the spider's perspective, first as a tiny version of himself, and then as what he thought the spider might see. Xander had an epiphany at that moment, though he didn't know to call it that at the time. He just remembered thinking something new. Although he could imagine being small and looking the way the spider did, he really had no idea what the spider was thinking or even if—or how—the spider thought at all. He glanced around at the other children and knew it was the same with them. He didn't know, couldn't know, what they were thinking.

The spider crawled onto his bare leg and stopped. Not having learned to fear it, he gently scooped it up to look more closely at it. It had a lot of legs and bore stripes in two different colors. He held it up to his face and examined it closely as it pivoted back and forth in his palm. He could just make out a faint glow surrounding it, and it mesmerized him until he was startled.

"Xander!" The teacher's panicked voice was almost a scream, and she bolted across the room toward him.

Xander quickly lowered his tiny hand and dropped the spider onto the floor near the corner. It started crawling back toward the wall, but not quick enough to avoid the teacher's shoe.

"Ugh! Nasty spider! Don't touch those, Xander. Spiders are bad."

Xander didn't understand exactly what she meant, but he understood that she had been afraid and that people didn't like what they were afraid of. She stood Xander up and inspected the bare parts of his arms and legs. Satisfied he had not been bitten, she took off her shoe and turned it over. Xander saw the smooshed spider. *No glow,* he thought.

"Eew," groaned the teacher, and Xander saw a disgusted look on her face as she hobbled to the sink to clean her shoe.

Xander thought about the spider again and wondered what it was thinking. He still didn't know the answer to that, but he knew then that it no longer had the same perspective, whatever that might have been. Also, he knew it had lost its glow.

Despite that experience being so brief, it made an obvious impact on Xander, as it began his search for the glow in other places.

At first, he started looking for other spiders or ants, but soon he realized he could see the glow on the family cat, Jinx. Xander had already learned what Jinx would tolerate and what would result in his slapping or nipping at him, so Xander would stroke Jinx's head with his fingers to feel his fur and the curve of his skull.

They were sitting by a window, and suddenly he saw his hand passing through a layer of light or shadow each time he lowered it to Jinx's head. He experimented by tickling the cat's neck, and when Jinx rolled over to nip at Xander's hand, Xander could see the glow move with him. It was faint, but he could see it clearly enough. The glow ran the length of Jinx's body and all around it, and extended only a little bit beyond the fur. From then on, Xander would spend every chance he had just sitting with Jinx and petting him, studying what looked like a cloud of energy surrounding him.

His mother eventually noticed that Xander was spending an inordinate amount of time petting and staring at Jinx, so she came and sat with them one day.

She was used to Xander's pensive behavior, so she didn't suspect anything when she saw him looking from her to Jinx and back to her, over and over, for several seconds.

Xander was fascinated; his mother also had a glow. He could see it, but it wasn't defined in the same way that Jinx's was. Rather than conform to the shape of her body, it hovered around her like a cloud... and it was colored, although he didn't think about the specific colors at the time, nor did he know their significance.

He didn't tell her about what he could see. Not that he was afraid to tell her; he was simply too mesmerized to mention it. From that moment on, he still spent a lot of time with the cat, but even more time watching his mom, and watching himself in the mirror. He would watch the energy clouds swirl and move about, the color combinations changing, becoming murky and then clearing.

He came to understand the power of people's thoughts and feelings over their clouds. The thoughts did influence the colors, but not nearly as much as the feelings. He knew, because once he understood the differences between them while watching others, he would practice with his own. By merely thinking a thought that was associated with an emotion, he found that his cloud's color combination might reflect a slight change that was barely noticeable. If he made an angry face, he might see a sparkle of red appear for an instant, but then it would be gone. However, if he felt angry or frustrated or elated, he sometimes found a subtle sign in his cloud's color combination representing those feelings.

Normally, his energy cloud was blue, sometimes lighter and sometimes darker. He had learned that he could glimpse a person's cloud and have a pretty good idea of what they were feeling, but not what they were thinking. Learning to read the clouds also taught him an important lesson about people… their words and actions did not always match their true emotions. That is how he learned how sarcasm, sympathy, and empathy worked. He quickly learned the value of interpreting the clouds. He knew by his mom's colors when a good time to ask her to buy something for him was, and also when he should just keep silent and hug her. He hugged her a lot in those days.

CHAPTER

TRACY sat on the other side of the desk from the doctor. She scanned the room out of boredom rather than interest, trying not to think about the narrow-minded schoolteacher who insisted she bring a doctor's note stating whether or not Xander had special needs and was well enough to be placed with the other children. *Normal* children. Plus, looking around the office gave her something to do while the Tier 1 citizen developed his judgment regarding her four-year-old son. She thought of the economic classes as tiers after years of listening to her father compare them to bottles of liquor. He viewed Tier 1 citizens—CEOs, doctors, lawyers, and the like—as the top-shelf bottles. They sat perched on high for the lower tiers to look straight up their asses, according to her father. Tracy knew this was a broad generalization, but it seemed to fit in this case. She was sure her occupation as an executive assistant placed her at no more than a Tier 2 status, but most likely at Tier 3 in the doctor's mind. *Oh, well,* she thought as she glanced at the shine from the balding head in front of her and then to his tight-lipped, concerned glare at the file on the desk in front of him.

He spoke to her without looking up.

"I see here you never had him vaccinated."

Tracy waited for him to look up at her for her response, but he continued scowling at the file as if he meant to intimidate the words on the paper into changing.

"That's right."

She remained calm for the moment. She had expected the standard questions, as well as the standard condescension.

After another minute of silence, she added, "What does that have to do at all with the fact that he doesn't often feel like talking. Maybe he just doesn't have anything to say."

"Ms. Noxx…"

Tracy rolled her eyes. *The condescension meter's pegged*, she thought.

"… all I'm saying is that at four, most children are talking, making eye contact, interacting with people… like normal."

That did it. Nothing could evaporate Tracy's patience like someone using the word "normal." *What is normal? Who decides? The Tier 1 citizens, of course*, she thought.

"And what does that even remotely have to do with Xander being vaccinated?"

She stood up, and planted both hands on the desk, and leaned across.

"Look, doctor, do you plan on diagnosing my son with anything? Because if he has… Asperger's or some form of autism or something, I'd rather you just write it up so I can begin ignoring it now."

She stood up and folded her arms. The doctor sighed a surrender and closed the file.

"Ms. Noxx, your son is physically healthy, but in my expert opinion, his mental state may require more testing. I simply don't have enough information with which to make a diagnosis."

Tracy shot right back at him, "*May* require? *You don't* have enough information or *there isn't* enough information?"

The doctor sighed again and, obviously restraining himself from saying something less than professional, replied, "I cannot make a diagnosis at this time."

"Fine." Tracy said. "Then I would appreciate it if you would be kind enough to put your *expert* opinion in a letter which I can give to his school."

Tracy fumed as she drove home, but she did her best to downgrade her anger to mere frustration as she pulled into the driveway. She knew Rebecca would be waiting with a barrage of questions. She also knew that Rebecca would agree with the doctor more than she would with Tracy. She would love to have Xander tested, too, since she didn't understand him any better than the doctor or Xander's teacher.

Tracy opened the door and had barely taken a step inside when Rebecca demanded information.

"Well? What did the doctor say?"

Tracy ignored the questions, walked the few steps to the breakfast bar, where she plopped down her purse and keys. Only then did she turn to look at her sister. Rebecca was twisted on the couch so she could see, her head stretched forward and her eyebrows trying to touch her scalp as she waited for answers. Xander was sitting cross-legged on the floor in front of the sofa. The television was on and playing some cartoon or another, but he was ignoring it as usual and looking at a children's book, one of several piled in front of him. Tracy looked at him and smiled, tilting her head to one side in adoration.

Rebecca had obviously waited long enough.

"Well?" she exclaimed, now looking perturbed rather than curious.

Tracy remained where she was near the bar.

"Well what?" she replied, shrugging.

Rebecca practically jumped up and walked around the sofa to confront Tracy.

"You know damn well what I'm talking about! What did the damn..."

They both looked over at Xander, who gave no acknowledgment he had heard or cared about the curse.

"Sorry. What did the darn doctor say? Do they want to run more tests on... *you know who?*"

They both glanced at Xander again, but only Tracy caught the fraction of a grin on him that appeared and then disappeared just as fast. Of course he was listening. She had known for some time he was already exceptionally gifted at multitasking. Not that it mattered whether or not he listened. Tracy had already planned on talking to him about what the doctor said. She saw no reason for keeping secrets from him or lying to him. She believed that treating children like people instead of some inferior and subordinate creatures was the right thing to do. Especially children as special as Xander. After all, were they not the future of the planet? And as gifted as Xander had already shown himself to be, there was no telling how much he would affect other people once he had truly come into his own.

"He said he was fine," Tracy finally replied.

Rebecca looked skeptical.

"Sure he did. I'll bet he wanted to test him some more, didn't he?"

Tracy ignored her sister's question.

"Thanks so much for keeping an eye on Xander for me, sis. Why don't you come over for dinner later on in the week?"

"Fine." Rebecca snapped. "Don't tell me." She walked back to the living room, grabbed her purse from the coffee table, and then knelt to hug and kiss Xander. "Bye, sweetie."

Xander turned his head just enough to watch his aunt stand, turn, and head for the door, and then he returned to his book.

Rebecca opened the door but stopped and spun her head toward Tracy.

"I love you, but you're very stubborn. Just make sure you're doing the best thing for Xander and not what's easy for you."

Rebecca exited and pulled the door shut to avoid Tracy's reaction, but Tracy stormed toward the door yelling, nonetheless.

"I am doing the best thing for Xander! I'm the only one!"

She realized she was yelling at the closed door and then turned to face Xander. He was looking toward her with a blank expression, but instead of looking at her face, his eyes seemed to be tracing her... going up one side to just above her head and then down the other side to the floor.

He is different, she thought, *but that's a good thing compared to what society considers normal.*

Yes, there was no denying he was different now. But not just different... special. From the time he was born, he had always seemed special, but not in any negative way. Tracy walked past Xander and sat down on the recliner so she could face him.

She sat there loving and adoring him. She said, "You are special. I knew it from the moment you were born. We all did."

Tracy realized she had teared up. She was just about to launch herself at Xander and wrap her arms around him when he stood up and walked over and gave her a hug. She squeezed him back. It was a long hug for him, lasting a full five seconds, so she let go as soon as she felt him release. He stopped to look into her eyes as he pulled away. His face still wore no expression, but Tracy felt his love and knew he was seeing her.

How does he always know what I'm feeling, Tracy thought?

She wondered if he was somehow able to sense her emotions. A second later and without a sound, Xander returned to his spot on the floor and continued reading.

CHAPTER 5

ONE sunny, muggy day in July when Xander was six, Tracy brought him to the community pool. Although they had been there a few times before, this was not a common excursion. Tracy wasn't as fascinated by crowds as Xander seemed to be, but she believed that parents should provide activities out of the home not just for educational activities, but also for social interaction. She also hoped bringing him more into contact with other kids his age might help him learn to better interact with them and, who knows, maybe with her as well.

Xander sat on the edge of the kiddie pool just a couple of feet in front of his mother and dangled his feet in the water. He would eventually go in all the way, but the contrast of the cold water on his legs with the heat from the humidity and the sun on the rest of his body was wonderful to him. Plus, he had a better vantage point from which to watch the other children and marvel at their energy clouds. A few parents were sitting on the edge as he was, coaching or playing with their own kids, but Xander watched the kids. He saw his mother and sometimes other adults every day, but he didn't often see other children outside of the few hours in preschool. There were four other boys and girls in the kiddie pool, and their energy clouds were colored with combinations of blue, pink, and orange. They were all very different from his own, which was predominantly blue. The only slight distraction from his current enjoyment was his water wings. The creases and corners of the inflated plastic scratched him as they rubbed his skin with the slightest movement of his arms. He was pulling one of the points out of his underarm when a shadow blocked part of the sunlight on his legs and he looked up to see that another child had moved directly in front of him.

Xander did not remember seeing her a moment before, so she must have just come in the pool while he was focused on his water wing. The girl put her hands on the edge outside of each of Xander's legs and allowed her legs to float up behind her. For a moment, they only stared at each other. She had long blonde hair that all but covered the back of her pink bathing suit, but it was hard to tell just how long, since the bottom half was straightened by being wet. Her light brown eyes seemed large to Xander, even though she was squinting a little from the sun's brightness. Other than that, she wore no distinguishing expression.

Xander, on the other hand, was entranced by her, and his eyes opened wider than usual to show it. What held his attention more than her beauty was her energy cloud. It was almost all blue. It wasn't dark or light... just blue. True blue. It vibrated and swirled slowly and gracefully all around her.

"Blue." Her voice startled Xander. "You're blue."

Xander looked down at his skin first, then realized what she was saying. She was seeing his energy cloud.

"So are you," he said, and the girl grinned.

He had never known anyone else who could see energy clouds. Of course, he didn't know that since he hadn't told anyone, even his mother, that he could see them himself. He watched the girl scan his body with her beautiful eyes.

The girl pulled her feet up to the wall, pushed herself back from the edge, and then kicked off. She wasn't wearing water wings, but she was able to float on her back for a few seconds and then stand up. She walked to the steps, pulled her long hair out of her face, and flung it on her shoulders.

She walked up the steps, stopped, and turned to Xander. Her eyes scanned him once more, and she smiled again.

"Bye!" she said and walked quickly along the big pool toward some adults lounging in the sun.

"Did you make a new friend? She was very pretty."

Tracy's voice startled Xander out of his trance, and he glanced up at his mother, who was smiling at him like she had a secret.

"What was her name?"

Xander turned his head back to the lounging adults but didn't see the girl. He looked around the pool area and caught a quick glimpse of her blonde hair and pink bathing suit disappearing into the locker rooms. Xander realized he had only spoken a few words to her and only about her cloud. He felt a weird sensation in the pit of his stomach, a little like the time he had gulped down a glass of cold milk too quickly after being outside on a hot day, but this feeling was something new. He looked back up to his mother with what must have looked to her like a sad face, because she tried to match it.

"Awww. Don't worry, honey. I'm sure she'll be back."

Xander turned his attention back to the locker rooms. He watched and waited for the girl, but she never reappeared. The weird feeling remained but had changed. Now he felt like he was starving. Even after his mother took him home, his stomach felt empty, and he felt just like his stomach.

The next couple of weeks brought more sun and warm weather. Xander noticed that he still sometimes felt the empty feeling he had at the pool when the girl had disappeared. The feeling remained with him, barely noticeable, but there. He did his best to ignore it and continued to ask his mother to take him to the pool.

They didn't go every day, but at least several times each week. Every time, Xander would plant himself on the edge of the pool while Tracy read nearby. He endured the discomfort of his water wings and would sit there, kicking his feet out and back from the edge, enjoying the cold water and, for the first few visits, scanning the pool and poolside every few minutes, looking for the girl with the blue energy cloud. By the end of the second week, he gave up his search and went back to watching the other children. Every once in a while, he would get his hopes up when he caught sight of a pink bathing suit or a small head of long blonde hair, but it was never her, and he eventually stopped thinking about her. Then one day, the empty feeling went away altogether.

CHAPTER 6

THE next couple of years convinced Tracy to make a change. She was scowling as she read through the document she had recently printed. It was one of many she had printed over the past few months. The documents provided information on homeschooling, and she had them spread out in piles on the table in front of her. Of course she had heard of the concept of homeschooling but was not familiar with anything but the basic idea of teaching Xander at home, in a safe, judgment-free environment. Not that it seemed to affect Xander as much as it did Tracy. After watching what happened time and again in public school while he attended his first- and second-grade classes, she was the one who worried that he was being singled out by the teachers and, in some cases, by other children for being different. Xander didn't seem to be bothered by much. *But that's how some introverts are*, Tracy told herself.

Xander was sitting by the TV, ignoring it in favor of his books and occasionally looking up at his mother to check on her cloud. He had just started understanding that he could not only see it, but could feel it from a distance and, sometimes, he could sense when it changed.

At the moment, her cloud was swirling rapidly with oranges and yellows. It looked to Xander like smaller rivers continuously joining and then splitting off again. He already knew the word frustration and knew that's what she was currently feeling. When her cloud looked like this, it was best to let her be. It would not last long.

He returned to his book. Reading never ceased to fascinate him, even when the topic he was reading about did not. His mother had made it a habit to explain how things work, so when she taught him to read, she had also explained how his brain worked with his eyes to recognize the letters, combine the sounds to form words, and match a meaning to the words. Xander had extrapolated on his own that his brain also matched a meaning to a group of words. He also thought it amazing that his brain could be doing that while also allowing him to learn the information in the books he read. He loved learning in any way, but especially through books. He would be content sitting on the floor with his books for as long as his mother would allow. He could go to the bathroom without disturbing her too much, and he would talk to her and risk cutting his reading time short by asking her to help him only with an exceptionally long or new word. He would even ignore hunger pangs in favor of more reading time and did his best to make his glances at her cloud discreet so she wouldn't think he needed something from her.

Tracy had begun separating some of the documents to help her determine which homeschooling method would be the best for Xander and the most feasible for her to deliver, when she was interrupted by a familiar knock on the door. She continued to review a piece of paper as she walked to the door.

She unlocked and opened it for her sister and then returned to the table as Rebecca walked in.

"Hi," Tracy said.

"Good morning to you too, sunshine," her sister said sarcastically.

Rebecca was dressed in a gray, smart-looking business suit with her "Rebecca Sampson, Corporate Sales" nametag prominently displayed on the left breast of her jacket. She closed the door and bee-lined to the coffeepot, giving Tracy a two-handed hug on the shoulders and a quick peck on the cheek as she past her. She poured a mug of coffee, grabbed the dirty spoon next to the coffeepot, retrieved the creamer from the refrigerator door, and sat down at the table.

"Hi, sweetie," she said to Xander as she doctored her coffee.

Xander glanced up at her in acknowledgment, looked above her to see her cloud, and then returned to his book. Rebecca shook her head and shifted her attention back to her coffee. She was used to feeling puzzled by Xander's lack of interaction and strange behavior. Part of the reason she thought he needed special attention was that he rarely made eye contact with her. In fact, he often seemed more preoccupied with looking above or around her body, as if he couldn't look directly at her.

Rebecca looked at the papers on the table and then picked up the closest page.

"What are you doing?" she asked Tracy.

Tracy sighed and stopped reading to look at her sister, who always seemed impatient.

"I'm researching how to homeschool Xander."

Rebecca shook her head and looked disappointed.

"No," Tracy said, her voice elevating. "I am sick and tired of my son being treated like he's inferior or contagious or... or... something. Just because he isn't a little chatterbox like they expect, except when he had questions and, God forbid, actually wants to learn something substantial, there must be something wrong with him!"

She sat down and continued her reading, although her frustration was preventing her from concentrating. Rebecca put the page she had been reading back on the table and took a loud sip of coffee, remaining silent otherwise.

After a few seconds, Tracy looked up at Rebecca once more.

"What?" Tracy demanded.

"Nothing" Rebecca answered, her eyes looking away from Tracy.

Tracy sighed and shuffled paper, too aggravated to read.

Rebecca's body relaxed and she said in a calm voice, "Let's say you're right and... you know who... is being picked on. How are you going to ensure he learns everything he's supposed to learn?"

Tracy pointed at Xander. "Look at him! He's been reading fluently for years... since he was four! Do you think he learned that at his daycare? At preschool? I can teach him the basics of what he needs to know and... well, you know him... he'll teach himself the rest."

Rebecca watched Tracy work her jaw muscles, something Tracy did when she was angry ever since they were kids.

"If you don't want to help, you can just sit there and drink your coffee or you're welcome to leave," Tracy snapped.

With that, Rebecca, remaining calm and sighing in surrender, picked up the page she had dropped and continued reading.

Xander couldn't help but listen to the conversation, which was a mere ten feet away, but he did so with indifference and flipped through the pages of the book in his hands. He already knew how his teachers felt about him based on how they treated him, but it didn't matter to him. He could see by their energy clouds they were often confused by him, and that made them frustrated... or afraid.

All that mattered to Xander was that he could continue learning, and he could do that at home just as easily, if not more easily, than he could at school. At home, he could learn at his own pace and he could use the internet. Also, his mother always had patience for him when he had questions, no matter how many he asked her. Without knowing the words, he knew his aunt was naturally, or at least habitually, adversarial to his mother, just as he knew his mother was defensive around his aunt. Although he didn't have a brother or a sister of his own, he understood the patterns of sibling rivalry by watching them.

His observation of the weird dynamic of some family members had already taught him another concept for which he did not yet know the word... irony. He could see by the energy clouds of his mother and her sister, for example, that they didn't much like each other. They tolerated each other because they were family and felt some obligatory loyalty that, for some strange reason, equated to a level of authentic love. He also knew that his aunt's love for him, although real, existed for the same reason— because they were relatives. He was only special to her and she to him because she was the aunt and he was the nephew. He knew that if he were not her nephew, she would see him as she did every other nonrelated child in the world. Just like he knew that if his mother and aunt were not sisters, they would not be friends and would not expend any energy to establish or maintain any kind of relationship.

Xander looked toward the kitchen at the energy clouds of the two women. His aunt Rebecca's had its usual dark orange hues because of her seriousness and stress. His mother's was similar, and that concerned Xander. Hers was usually light blue with swirls of pink and green mixed in. He put his book down, pushed himself up, and walked over and wrapped his arms around his mother's side. Rebecca tilted her head to one side and smiled at the gesture. Tracy looked down at her son as she hugged him back and leaned her head on his with a smile of her own. Xander closed his eyes and imagined his own blue energy cloud hugging his mother's cloud. After a few seconds, he could feel her body soften and relax, and he knew that her cloud was changing also. He looked up at her face and then above her to confirm that her cloud had changed, gave her a quick grin, and then pulled away and returned to the living room and his books.

Tracy watched him walk back and sit down to dive back into the book he was reading. She knew he would finish that one quickly and immediately start on a new one. Yes, he was different. Special. But not in any way that was negative. He was the kind of special that she would like to see rub off on other people… maybe even on the whole world.

CHAPTER

I T didn't take long for Tracy to think that even homeschooling may not be the best learning environment for Xander. She had tried two different programs for a few months each and had settled on a third one, which they used for the remainder of third and most of fourth grade. This particular program was directed by a virtual administration and consisted of a set curriculum and routine field trips and activities for the group of children in the area who were also participating in the same program. It was more flexible than public schools, but still had some set parameters.

There were fourteen kids in the group, with ages ranging from seven to thirteen. Having turned ten halfway through the year, Xander fell close to the middle of the range. The academic portion of the program was problematic only in that Xander wasn't challenged, at least not for very long at any one time. Whenever he encountered a new concept, his progress in that area would slow for a short time, but once he grasped the concept, he would breeze through whatever else on that topic that came his way.

Social interaction with his peer group was another matter. He didn't usually have problems, but it was clear that he either didn't quite get the expected social exchanges with other people or he chose not to follow them. Tracy thought there was more truth to the latter theory. As for Xander himself, he understood the expectations of his peers perfectly, as well as those of the parents. It wasn't that he was being rebellious; it was just that he didn't naturally think of or consider their expectations until it was too late.

He sometimes would understand and be amused by jokes but not laugh out loud. If another child in the group would be hurt horsing around or on accident during an activity, his face wouldn't show any emotion and he would, at times, be criticized as not caring. Usually, one of the parents would coddle the hurt child and say things like, "Are you okay, dear?" while some of the other children would show pain or sorrow on their faces. Xander didn't understand their reactions. He would think, *They weren't hurt, so why was there an expectation for them to look, sound, or feel hurt?* Empathy was a word he had looked up one time when a parent, who noticed his expressionless face after she had informed him and the other children that one of the kids from the group had broken his arm, informed him that he had none. He understood the definition and that it was, for some reason, an expectation by most people, but it didn't make sense to him. *Why should I choose to feel sad or bad or sorry for other people? What would that help? Wouldn't the world be a better place if everyone who wasn't experiencing some sort of hurt chose to feel good instead?*

Xander knew there were times when he also felt pain or sadness, but those moments when he couldn't choose otherwise were enough for him, and he wondered why he should choose to feel that way for other people. Of course, even when he did feel bad, his face didn't always match his feelings, and because he didn't look the way other people expected him to at certain times, they criticized him for it.

He spoke to his mother about the subject once that year, and her response was something he would never forget. He asked, "Why are people okay with feeling bad when they can choose to feel good?"

After thinking about it for a few seconds, she replied, "I guess it's because people feel they have to react or respond to things. They have to do something. It's just human nature."

Xander nodded, but he was still puzzled.

I'm human, too, he thought.

CHAPTER

THE clear sign to Tracy that she was at least ready to experiment with the unorthodox concept of unschooling came to her on a wet, fall day after one of the homeschooling activities at a community park. Tracy and Xander were on their way home when, after the air from the vents was at last delivering some semblance of warmth, Xander unzipped his coat and folded down the collar that had been guarding his face and ear lobes from the rain and wind. Tracy glanced at her son to see if his color was returning after his exposure to the cold.

"Oh my God, Xander! What happened to your face?"

Xander pointed at the brake lights in front of them which had suddenly illuminated and seem to be rapidly approaching. "Watch the road, Mother," he said in his normal, calm voice.

Tracy hit the brakes and looked forward, then swiveled her head several times between the road and Xander. He was facing frontward, and his face was expressionless yet was adorned with a large, purple scrape that was partially filled with blood and dirt.

"What happened?" she demanded.

Tracy knew that a couple of the other kids didn't always treat Xander nicely and, in fact, were just plain mean at times. In the past, they had resorted only to name calling and other verbal attacks, but Tracy wouldn't put it past a couple of the older ones to use their size and Xander's gentle demeanor to elevate their teasing to the physical realm.

She realized she had sounded stern when she asked that last question and followed up with a softer tone. "Did you trip or something?" she asked, doing her best to give the situation and the other kids the benefit of the doubt.

Xander had never seen a value in lying. It just did not make sense not to tell the truth, so he told her. "Steve pushed me" he said, still looking forward.

Tracy's original suspicion confirmed, she no longer tried to conceal her anger. "Augh! I knew it! I hate those bullies. I should turn around and go right to his house and tell his mom."

"Please don't," Xander pleaded, facing his mother as he said the words.

She looked at him, and as soon as he saw the angry red start to dissipate from her cloud, he faced forward again.

"It doesn't matter," he said.

Xander replayed the incident in his mind. He chose not to make a habit of dwelling in the past, but he also knew it was okay to think about things even if they resurrected emotions so long as he didn't stay attached to those emotions.

He had been walking around the perimeter of the park where the homeschool group had decided to meet. It was a pretty park, with a lot of thick, green grass and many trees. Toward the center, there was a small pond with some ducks and a wooden playground with ropes to climb, poles to slide, tunnels to hide in, swings, and a curly slide. He wasn't deliberately trying to be alone or stand out in any way, he was just not interested in running around in the rain. He also didn't feel like playing whatever make-believe game some of the bigger boys had invented, especially because they often involved overly aggressive versions of tag. Nor did he want to feed or chase the ducks. Instead, he sought pleasure in walking the paved walkway that wound its way through the trees near the outer edges of the park.

Despite the light rain, the mugginess that created a coat of glossy sweat on his exposed skin, and the communities of gnats that saw it as an invitation to swarm him every few yards, he felt comfortable in the setting. He walked with his head bowed and his hands in his front pockets, letting his mind wander and his senses explore his surroundings. Even with his hood up, he was able to enjoy the various sounds of rain, birds, traffic, and even the other kids. He watched the occasional squirrel scurry around the base of a tree and he inhaled mossy scents. As he reached a lengthy curve in the sidewalk, he suddenly decided to bypass it and cut straight across the grass.

He had taken four steps and was about halfway to the other side of the curve when he was shoved hard from behind. He had started to turn his head to the right when he was hit again, hard against his shoulder blades. He wasn't able to completely free his left hand from his pocket and absorbed the fall with his knees, right hand, and left cheek. Despite the grass, there was enough coarse dirt and pebbles to scrape his face and stain his knees. Had the ground been more solid, his right wrist would have hurt even worse than it did.

His left hand finally found its way out of his pocket, and he turned himself over to sit on the ground, pulling back his hood to face the audience of four boys who stood over him. They were all laughing, but Xander could see from their clouds that they weren't all happy. Three of them, in fact, had agitated clouds with charcoal-colored streams. They were exhilarated and scared, but Xander could tell they were more worried about looking cool than about how they actually felt inside. The cloud belonging to the fourth boy was a gross-looking stew of brown and red. Steve was the name of the cloud's owner. He was standing in front of the other boys and was obviously the one who had shoved Xander. Steve was laughing hard and pointing down at Xander.

"You dropped something," Steve said, glancing back at the other boys to ensure they were in on his joke.

Xander had been surprised by the push, but not just because it was from behind. Steve had been escalating his taunting of Xander for a couple months but had never touched him before.

Xander understood this was a pivotal moment in their relationship. He could choose to let fear settle in and lie in wait for Steve or the mere thought of Steve to summon it, or he could detach himself from the incident, which was now in the past. He knew that if he allowed it to happen, tears would immediately well up in his eyes, and his face would contort to express pain and sorrow. But Xander didn't like choosing to feel fear, hurt, or other negative feelings. He wanted to feel good, so he chose the latter choice and detached from the shove. He remained expressionless, allowing his face and body to relax, easing the pain in his face, wrist, and knees. He gazed up at Steve and then to Steve's energy cloud. Xander visualized his own cloud returning to his normal blue and expanding outward to make contact with Steve's cloud.

"What are you looking at, you freak?" Steve said.

Steve was confused. He had expected submission by this clearly weaker kid, but instead of crying and submitting, Xander merely looked at Steve like nothing was wrong. Steve had planned to make fun of Xander amidst his tears while he begged Steve to leave him alone. It always made Steve feel good about himself, like he was big and strong, powerful, when he could overpower someone else. But it wasn't working this time. He did not feel strong or powerful. This smaller kid was on the ground at Steve's feet, and even bleeding, but he didn't look like he felt hurt or afraid... or powerless.

Meanwhile, Xander could see his own blue cloud mix in with Steve's cloud. The blue swirls not quite blending to change Steve's color, but it did lighten the shade. In any case, the difference in Steve's cloud was too much for him.

"Come on, guys," he said, and with a wave of his arms walked around Xander and on down the path.

The other boys each made quick eye contact with Xander as they passed him. He did not see joy on their faces or in their clouds.

Xander sat on the ground for another minute, looking around him at the grass and the trees and appreciating the different perspective he had from down there. Then he stood up, brushed off his hands, knees, and cheek, and walked on in the same direction as the other boys as if nothing had happened.

His mother's voice brought his attention back to the present.

"Of course it matters," Tracy replied. "Nobody has the right to push other people around. Especially when there's no reason to do it and the person is... well, smaller than you. He's just a bully."

Xander shook his head and sighed. "He's just afraid... like everyone else."

Tracy was not sure what to think of Xander's answer. "Afraid? Afraid of what?"

Xander thought for a second and then replied, "Afraid of being alone. Afraid of being the one who will be picked on. Afraid that he's not good enough."

Tracy had to ask, "Good enough for what?"

Xander glanced sideways and was pleased to see that his mother's cloud no longer had any red in it. He faced forward again. "Good enough not to care about what other people think."

Tracy's jaw dropped slightly, but otherwise, her face was as expressionless as Xander's. *Wow*, she thought.

"Xander" she began, "you have more insight into life at ten than most people will ever have."

Xander contemplated his mother's words for a few seconds. "I hope that's not true," was all he said.

He thought these so-called insights were simple, and it was hard for him to fathom that not everyone understood them. Then another thought occurred to him. They do understand them; at least their subconscious does. It's just that, like Steve, they too are afraid.

CHAPTER

Rebecca stared at her sister, flabbergasted, as she did her best to come to terms with what she had just learned. She understood that, as crazy as it sounded, it wasn't every parent's goal to have their child attend college these days, but she assumed those were the minority who had delusions of grandeur that their children would be successful entrepreneurs. Most of the young adults she was familiar with who had not gone on to college were working limited or dead-end jobs, but at least they still had potential for careers. *Once they pull their heads out of their asses, that is*, Rebecca said to herself.

It was bad enough that Tracy thought she could do as well as the public school system when she elected to join the ranks of the other rebellious parents who couldn't handle their kids being uncomfortable. They thought they were doing their kids a favor by rescuing them from whatever challenge they were facing in public schools, but Rebecca knew they were actually hurting their kids by not letting them experience those small victories every kid faces and needs. To make matters even worse, and what shocked Rebecca into silence, was that Tracy had just informed her that she was stopping whatever homeschooling efforts she was making for Xander and allowing him to do nothing. Rebecca knew that was not quite accurate, though. What her sister had said was that she was going to allow Xander to *unschool*, which, to Rebecca, sounded a lot like allowing him to do nothing and to learn nothing.

Tracy continued to eat her salad, seeming very comfortable with her decision and with her sister's silence and obvious objection. She had done her research. Unschooling was not only the only reasonable option for Xander at this point, she knew it was the right thing. Plus, it was a proven concept, though it had never been labeled a legitimate educational method. Many successful people throughout history had little or no formal education. Besides, Xander had always been a quick learner, whether through reading or, incredibly enough, through his own insightful observations. Also, and most importantly in Tracy's opinion, she would not have to worry about teachers or other students mistreating her son.

Xander sat between the two at the small round table in the restaurant. Though he and his mother didn't often eat out, when they did, they usually came to this place, since it was close to home and inexpensive. Plus, his mother liked it because she said they used fresh ingredients. She tried to eat healthily and to teach Xander to do the same, although she sometimes gave in to both his requests and her desire to indulge. He had ordered fish, rice, and steamed vegetables from the lunch menu and was munching a mouthful of green beans while he ignored the conversation at the table and glanced around at the other patrons... and their energy clouds. He was told people thought it was rude to stare, though he didn't understand why. People were interesting, and their clouds more so. He thought it ironic that people did not want other people watching them when, by watching them, people would have a better understanding of each other. Fear again. And fear only seems to create more fear. Xander recognized his thoughts but didn't get attached to them, and so they did not bother him. He merely watched and learned.

Tracy had almost finished her salad entrée by the time Rebecca finally spoke.

"Tracy, help me understand," she said with a patronizing tone.

She was very conscious of Xander's presence, her eyes darting to him and back to Tracy. She chose her words with care.

"Just how is... learning... supposed to take place?"

Tracy sat back in her chair, put her fork down, and wiped her mouth with her napkin. She said very calmly, "You don't have to talk about him like he's not right next to you."

Rebecca glanced at Xander, wiped her own mouth, and adjusted herself in her chair, seeming uncomfortable as Tracy continued.

"Xander has absolutely no problems in the learning arena, and you know he's above average in all of his subjects. More than above average," she said, smiling at Xander.

"But unschooling?" Rebecca said the word like it was sour in her mouth. "I mean, what is that? No plan, no curriculum… no goals? And who's going to teach him advanced subjects like algebra and geometry and chemistry?"

Tracy was glad that she'd prepared herself for this conversation. She knew her sister and had expected her to be adversarial to the unschooling idea just as she had been when Tracy had told her about her earlier decision to homeschool Xander. But Tracy had done her homework and, for once, was able to stand up to her sister with the calm confidence of someone who knew she was right.

"First of all, I said there was no *predetermined* curriculum. Xander will come up with his own curriculum as he decides what he wants to learn. As for the advanced subjects…" Tracy said the last two words with the same contempt with which her sister said unschooling, but then her face changed as she decided to change tactics. "… what is your title? At work. At your job. What is your title?"

Rebecca was clearly caught off guard. She blinked and shook her head, confused.

"Uh… I'm the corporate sales manager. But what does that…"

Tracy cut her off, "Are you successful? I mean, do you think you have a successful career?"

Rebecca scowled at her sister, sat up tall, and answered while trying to control her volume.

"Considering I work for one of the top three business system services in the state, yes, I would say I'm successful."

Tracy wore a small, satisfied grin.

"Tell me, Mrs. Corporate Sales Manager, exactly how much algebra, geometry, and chemistry did you have to use to get your job? How much do you use on a daily basis?"

Rebecca continued to scowl at her sister.

"I happen to have a bachelor's degree! And I had to learn all those subjects to get it!"

Tracy raised her eyebrows, amused. "I'm sorry, what's your degree in?"

Rebecca's scowl changed to a frown. "English," she said, and she lowered her eyes to her plate to avoid Tracy's smirk.

Tracy was quick with a follow-up question. "And did you use your degree to land your successful career? Hell, did you even need it?"

Rebecca's eyes widened and she pursed her lips as she motioned with her head toward Xander. "Tracy... language."

Tracy maintained her grin. "Oh, Xander's heard me say hell before. Answer the question, Rebecca."

Rebecca sighed and slumped her shoulders, defeated. "No, okay. I didn't need my degree to get the job."

Tracy sat back, relaxed and satisfied. She knew she had just won a small victory. It wasn't often she won an argument with her sister, but she didn't want to give her time to regroup, so she continued her platform.

"Unschooling will allow Xander to learn what interests him. If he needs to learn something I can't teach him, he can enroll in an online course or learn it from a book. These days, he can probably learn it through a video on YouTube. We'll be fine. He'll be fine."

Rebecca stared at her sister with a small amount of contempt. She was not used to not being right—or at least to not having a good argument to make her sound right. Right now though, she was stumped. She liked tradition and convention, and this unschooling concept was anything but. She believed Xander would have a hard time fitting into society if he didn't take the same steps as everyone else.

Rebecca's cellphone vibrated on the table and she picked it up, pushing a button with her thumb. She stood up as she blotted her mouth with her napkin.

"I've got to run."

She dropped her napkin next to her plate and reached for her purse hanging from her chair.

"My turn to pay," Tracy said.

"Thank you." Rebecca transferred her purse from the chair to her shoulder and faced Tracy.

"Look... I just don't want my nephew to be limited."

Tracy grinned and answered, "That's the beauty. He'll actually be unlimited since he won't need any rigid curriculum."

"If you say so."

Rebecca hugged her sister and then moved past her to Xander. She bent over and kissed his head. "Bye, sweetie."

"Bye," replied Xander, looking up at her with no particular expression.

"Love you two," she said as she turned and left.

"Love you," Tracy said.

Tracy watched her sister walk across the small restaurant and out the door. She sighed and looked over at Xander, who seemed to be looking just over her head. He dropped his eyes to meet hers once he realized her head had swiveled to face him.

"We're going to be just fine," she said reassuringly, though Xander knew by the nervous vibration in her cloud that she was saying it more to reassure herself than him.

Xander wasn't worried. He understood the concept of unschooling. When his mother first explained it to him, he wondered how public schools were actually created and why people would think that everyone needed to know the exact same things. *Kids aren't robots*, he thought, *so why were they being taught to think alike?* He wasn't the same as everyone else, and he didn't want to be. Besides, once he learned to read, he could use books or the internet to learn anything else he wanted or needed. He had read enough to understand that having a similar foundation in knowledge was good, but he didn't see the benefit to forcing children to learn things they may never need. Also, public schools and even homeschooling rarely taught him about the things he thought were important. Things like energy clouds and understanding people. Things like how to be happy.

CHAPTER 10

Unschooling for Xander went even better than Tracy had expected. Not only did he have the freedom to learn what he wanted to learn when he wanted to learn it, but it relieved Tracy of the responsibility of having to research and find a suitable curriculum.

Tracy had thought the downside of unschooling might be the lack of social interaction with other kids Xander's age, but she found ways around that challenge. She found that she and Xander were welcomed to participate in many homeschooling groups during their field trips and learning activities, but without any expectation of attending a certain number of them. That was perfect; Tracy and Xander could visit one on a trial basis to see the dynamics of the group and whether Xander and the group were a good fit.

As unschooling became more popular, Tracy was able to find more of those groups to try out. They were often helpful, at least for Tracy, because she didn't have to try to explain the unschooling concept to other parents, so many of whom would look at her with a patronizing smile and say things like, "That's so interesting." She knew some of them were judging her, since they would find a reason to abruptly stop their conversations with her.

The unschooling also worked well from Xander's point of view. It allowed him to do what he loved most, which was to read. Only now, he didn't have to stop very often. Also, he could focus on whatever subject he wanted to learn, regardless of whether anyone else thought it too mature for him. He loved reading fact-based books, but he enjoyed other genres as well, especially fantasy and science fiction. He found that they taught him as much about people and relationships as the nonfiction did about biology, history, or economics. If only his mother could understand that. He knew she thought it important that he learn things through more practical methods too—namely, social interaction with kids his own age. He was okay with that and didn't resist participating in unschooling activities with others, as he and his mother were usually like-minded when it came to their synergy with a certain group.

Eventually, Tracy and Xander found a group they liked and began to regularly attend events and activities with that group. Tracy felt comfortable talking with several of the other parents, including a couple of fathers, about various topics, although whatever they talked about normally circled around to the reasons they had chosen to unschool their kids. Sometimes it was dissatisfaction with the public schoolteachers or administrations, but other times it was to break their kids away from the control of mainstream society.

One set of parents, George and June Waller, were very outspoken about the latter reason. George and June had virtual jobs that often allowed them both to participate in the unschool activities with Grace, their nine-year-old daughter. George and June were older than most of the other parents there, in their mid-forties, and seemed to seek out opportunities to loudly express their strong opinions about how the government controlled the masses with fear by whatever means it had at its disposal, such as the military and the media. According to George and June, the government also used other tactics to control the populace, like pharmaceuticals and vaccinations, but they almost always talked about the educational system. They proclaimed that it was outdated, not only in the curriculum, but in its pedagogy. They believed teachers shouldn't be teaching to the slowest kid in class, nor should they go too fast for any of them. They also believed, like Tracy, that many of the mandatory subjects were irrelevant or just plain unnecessary.

Tracy agreed with most of what the Wallers ranted about, but listened and nodded without saying much. Mostly because, once they were on their soapbox, they tended to go on until the end of the day's activity and it was time to say goodbye. Tracy didn't mind too much. She was just glad she didn't have to defend her parenting choices to them. Also, the other kids didn't pick on Xander, though he still usually ended up wandering around by himself.

Xander liked the group well enough. He had spoken to most of the other kids in the group at some time or another, and they all seemed to accept him. At least enough to not bother him. That was fine with him, just as it was with Tracy.

In total, they spent more than three years with that group. A few of the other kids and parents came and went, but the activities and meet-ups continued.

Tracy eventually became involved with the leadership of the group, which focused on researching ideas for the activities. It was easy to plan the meet-ups, which were usually outdoors, but it was a challenge to settle on activities at times due to the age range of the children in the group. While there were many parks, lakes, festivals, and such outside, determining an indoor activity wasn't as easy. Another challenge was to find activities and venues in different areas so no family had to constantly drive more than the others. Since she shared the planning responsibility with a few other parents on the leadership team, it didn't overburden her and she was able to stick with it. It also gave her a much-needed social outlet, if only for the hour or so during the group's meetings.

She had prepared for one of the planning meetings with the leadership team by researching museums. She was proud of herself. Not only had she printed color flyers with highlighted exhibits and activities offered at several museums across the three counties where the group families lived, but she also created a spreadsheet that compared the museums' locations, exhibits and activities. The group was impressed by her energy, and the members agreed the group would try to visit them all.

Tracy recommended they start with the science museum in the adjacent county. It was a hands-on museum and would appeal to all ages. The group agreed and set a date for the visit. Tracy was excited when she shared the news with Xander. Despite his unemotional reception to the idea, she knew him enough to know that he would welcome the experience because he would have an opportunity to learn something new.

CHAPTER 11

TRACY could not have planned the field trip to the science museum any better. The sky was gray and the air was damp and heavy but lacking the release even a light rain would provide, so an inside activity was optimal. Also, the parking lot was unseasonably empty and the group's convoy found spaces relatively close to the entrance. Tracy was hopeful the semi-vacant lot meant the museum would not be packed, and she was not disappointed. The museum was not crowded, even though it was a weekday, which could easily lure busloads of public school classes. It seemed to Tracy that the stars were aligned to make the trip a complete success.

The leadership team had decided on a few group activities, as well as some free time when the families or older kids could wander around the museum by themselves. They all attended the planetarium and the laser dome together, and walked through the History of Science Hall before discussing an exit rendezvous, synchronizing their watches, and splitting up.

Tracy and a couple of other moms continued to walk together toward the Hands-on Exhibition Hall. Xander didn't understand all of the exhibits, but he was fascinated nonetheless. He was able to participate in the building areas, basic biology, and other exhibits recognized by all ages. Tracy followed Xander around the room, content with watching her son's endless interest in everything.

Xander felt a small and sudden chill in his chest at the exact moment an odd sound caught his attention. He cocked his head to listen and then turned in place to identify the source. About 30 feet to his left, a group of kids and adults were gathered around a large glass ball that looked like it contained a 360-degree lightning storm. Each time one of the people surrounding the globe touched the glass, a streak of lightning would connect with the same spot on the inside and linger there, arcing and flashing, almost appearing to dance with the person touching the glass.

Tracy could see her son's obvious interest, smiled, and said, "Let's go check that out."

She took the lead and they walked toward the sphere. After a few steps, Xander stopped, not because of apprehension of the exhibit or the people, but because he was losing his view. His short stature sometimes allowed him to see over people better from a distance. Tracy watched him craning his neck upward, then grabbed his hand and weaved through the crowd toward the front, where the smaller kids were watching and interacting with the sphere.

"Better?"

Xander nodded without breaking his gaze at the spectacle, and Tracy moved closer.

Xander's eyes widened and he noticed something peculiar as he watched the crowd interacting with the storm sphere. Each time someone touched the glass, an audible buzz followed the connection between the person and the lightning streak. That was the sound that had caught his attention just after he felt the earlier chill. He felt for that feeling again and found it, ever so slight, along with the buzz whenever a new connection was made with the lightning.

Tracy asked, "Wanna touch it?"

Xander did not answer right away, so Tracy waited, not wanting to push him.

"Not yet," Xander replied after about ten seconds, still staring ahead.

Something else was happening. Xander stared intently at the sphere and at the connections forming and disappearing as the people moved around it. He wondered how their own energy clouds would look, so he focused on looking for them.

At first, he didn't notice anything unusual about them. They were of various color combinations and sizes, and all moving differently, but as his eyes followed the cloud of one individual and then another as they each touched the globe, he saw something happen.

At the precise moment the connection with the lightning was made, the energy cloud of the person touching the globe seemed to expand and brighten, ever so slightly. For some reason, Xander started to associate the change in their clouds with the sensation he was feeling rather than with the connection with the lightning.

He wanted to be sure, so he turned toward his mother and said, "Okay."

Tracy grinned at him and walked them around the sphere until she found an opening where they could be next to the glass. Once there, Xander did not immediately reach for the glass, but stood staring at the lightning for a moment. Now he was able to easily feel the changes to the clouds of the people around him and could, without even looking or listening for the buzz, tell when someone was touching the glass. He finally placed his own hand on the glass. He found the connection between the lightning and his hand interesting, but nowhere near as fascinating as the internal feeling he was experiencing with the energy clouds.

After reading the small information plate about the sphere, he learned that it was called a plasma ball. He also understood that the lightning inside the plasma ball was a form of energy. He thought of the clouds and the lightning and realized that they were essentially the same. He had even seen some clouds moving much faster, with streaks of color moving similar to the lightning.

It's all energy, he thought.

Xander felt something else odd but didn't associate it with anything. His mother said, "I think it's time to go, Xander."

He looked up at his mother, who had one hand on the glass and one on her forehead and, aside from the smallest tinge of a few tan specks in her cloud, thought she looked fine.

They made the rounds to the nearby members of the unschool group, saying goodbyes. Tracy apologized for leaving early, but she had a headache.

As they exited the museum and headed for the parking lot, Xander was surprised that he could still feel changes to people's energy clouds. At first, he thought they might still be close enough to the plasma ball, but then realized he was feeling small changes to the clouds around him. The clouds in the sky had changed, too, giving way to sun and more heat, and as he fastened his seat belt, he felt sleepy due to the combination of walking through the museum and the warmth of the car.

Xander thought about the plasma ball and the energy clouds he was able to feel. Then he reached out with his attention to try and sense his own cloud and then his mother's. He was easily able to feel them both. As they pulled out of the parking lot and onto the street, Xander closed his eyes and wondered how he could feel them when they weren't making the connection to the lightning.

Is there other energy around that I can't see?

He tried to imagine what that would look like as the car pulled onto the freeway. He fell asleep to the smooth vibrations that come with speed and a smooth road as he thought, *What if it's all connected?*

CHAPTER 12

OVER the next couple of years, Xander continued to unschool, and he and Tracy remained active with the group. Every once in a while, Tracy would worry that Xander might not be learning everything he should be learning or feel guilty about not having a set curriculum, but then she would catch Xander researching an advanced subject or using vocabulary he didn't learn from her and she would feel better. She would also remind herself that all the things they teach in school are not necessarily for the benefit of the students, but to create predictable creatures to fill the lower tiers that make up the bulk of society.

Tracy insisted on at least a biweekly check-in with Xander to ask him what he'd been reading and learning, and if he had any questions. Tracy documented the check-ins and kept her handwritten records in a file folder in date order, partially because her initial research indicated that documentation was a best practice in unschooling, but mostly because it would appease the people she knew who were stuck in convention and tradition, like her sister. Even Rebecca seemed to feel better about the idea knowing there was some documentation. Plus, Tracy always enjoyed talking with Xander about what he had been reading, and he never failed to impress her with the topics that interested him. Although she would have been happy if he was interested in what was common for kids his age, she was ecstatic that he seemed more interested in learning about sociology and psychology, and not just from ancient text books, but from current sources as well. Tracy thought it was much better than him spending all his time playing online video games like some of the other kids in their group.

She was also impressed that he seemed to grasp just about any concept he came across, and when he didn't, he either used the internet or, once in a while, asked her for clarification.

Some of Tracy's fears were greatly relieved and her faith in unschooling validated after a conversation she had with Xander during one of their check-ins. He was just shy of turning thirteen but spoke with the vocabulary and maturity of someone much older. He and Tracy had deep conversations about a wide variety of topics, one of the most common about people—specifically about their thinking and behaviors.

Despite Tracy's routine disclaimer that she was no expert in any field, Xander often wanted her opinion on how and why people did the things they do. It was clear to Tracy that Xander was smart enough to know it was usually only her subjective thoughts she could give him, but he seemed to genuinely appreciate and respect her insight. Tracy savored those moments and dreaded the time when he would stop asking for her opinion.

They were sitting at the kitchen table, a plate of oatmeal chocolate chip cookies between them and each with a cup of herbal tea in front of them, as was their check-in routine. Tracy felt okay compromising their healthy diet like this, since Xander usually chose to drink water and tea instead of juice and soda and to eat the salads and stir fried vegetables she usually made for meals. They would usually sit for a few minutes, each starting on a cookie while waiting for their tea to cool. Eventually, Tracy would begin by asking Xander what he's been reading. She knew of any books she had seen him reading, but he did more of his reading on the internet. This time, Xander mixed it up by talking first.

"Mother..." he began and then paused, staring at Tracy but straight through her.

Tracy understood. He was processing. Forming and arranging his words to articulate his complex thoughts. She was accustomed to his pauses. She smiled, not to make fun or because of his expression, because he wasn't using one, but because she loved that he calls her *mother* instead of *mom*. She had not heard any of the other kids in the group use anything but *mom*. *Mother* made her feel special.

Xander's focus shifted back and he continued. "Why do people tend to make the same mistakes over and over?"

Tracy was still smiling. "What mistakes?"

"Choosing the wrong jobs, the wrong people to be with, the wrong things in their lives."

Although Xander spoke with his normal, calm, and serious tone, Tracy's imagination detected the smallest bit of sadness in his voice. But she knew better than to assume that's what he was feeling.

"What makes you think they make the wrong choices?" she asked.

"They're not happy." Xander said flatly. "At least most of them. It's obvious. They smile and pretend to be happy, but they always have to do something more. They always seem to need to buy or to make or to do the next thing. It's like they're chasing their happiness."

He paused again, but Tracy could tell by his blank gaze that he was processing and had not finished talking, so she waited. After a few seconds, he continued.

"Why don't they just choose to be happy?"

Now it was Tracy's turn to process. She cocked her head in thought and looked up to the light fixture that hung above the table. *Was he right? Did people simply choose not to be happy?* She knew her son was extremely insightful, but she also had to agree that it was obvious.

Of course he's right, she thought. In her experience, most people weren't usually happy unless they were looking forward to something or doing something to make themselves happy. Even she herself wasn't completely happy. She wondered whether she also chased happiness.

Why don't people just choose to be happy? she wondered.

She answered, but it was clear it was a guess on her part. "Maybe people have to be doing something to be happy. Maybe we have to create our own happiness."

That was plausible, she thought, but she wasn't certain, and her doubt grew as Xander shook his head.

"I don't think so. Adults say they don't want to work, but they do it anyway because they think they will be happy when they buy stuff or go on vacation. After they get the stuff, they think they need more or bigger stuff to be happy. On vacation, they taste happiness, because they don't have to work, but as soon as they return to work, they're not happy again. Then they think they'll be happy once they retire."

"Well, honey, all that stuff, vacations, and retirement, are what people need to make them happy." Tracy wasn't sure even she believed that to be true.

"But not all people. I read about people in other countries who have a lot less than people here and they seem happy. Some work and some don't. A lot of them are even unhealthy, but they seem happy." Xander sat back, pondering, and started eating another cookie.

Tracy stared at her son, not knowing what to say or even what she thought about what he said. He was right again. There are people who are happy, and not because they have a great job or lots of money; they're just happy. But Tracy knew those people were the clear minority. She was at a loss for how to answer her son's questions, at least without rationalizing or making up an answer, so she answered honestly.

"I don't know why people don't just choose to be happy, regardless of anything else. I guess it's because... they think they need something other than themselves to be happy."

Xander stopped chewing for a few seconds, pondering his mother's words.

He swallowed and said, "I think you're right."

Tracy looked up at the cat-shaped clock on the wall. They were going to an unschooling group meet-up at one of the nicer parks in the county, but it was about a thirty-minute drive, and they were supposed to meet there in an hour.

"Okay, Xanderman. Time to get ready to go."

Xander took a gulp of his tea, wiped the crumbs from his hands over his plate, and got up from his chair. He walked toward his bedroom, but stopped at the beginning of the hallway and turned back to his mother.

"I think it's silly."

"What's silly?" asked Tracy.

"Thinking we need something outside ourselves to be happy. Just choose to be happy. It's easy."

Tracy looked in awe at Xander.

"I think it's silly, too. Now go and get ready." Xander had a gift for clarity. Just choose to be happy. He was right. Although, in her opinion, not about the easy part.

CHAPTER

THEY arrived at the park right on time and were the first of the group to arrive. They were joined by several other families only a few minutes later and walked as a group to find a place for their blankets, coolers, and lawn chairs. The park was busy, but not overly crowded, and they chose a shady spot with a little sun and enough room for the late arrivers.

Although there were no formal rules, the group's practice was to sit together for a few minutes, catch up on the members' new happenings of interest, and introduce any new families. There happened to be one new family at this meet-up, the Carlsons. The Carlson family, at least the ones present, consisted of a mother and son. The mother introduced herself as Chrissy and her thirteen-year old son, David, and said she had learned about the group from its website. She told the group she and David were new to unschooling and were doing their due diligence to explore the dynamics of a dedicated group.

Chrissy Carlson's age was undeterminable. She looked like exhaustion had not only caught up with her but had settled in for a time. She was friendly, but was not quiet and reserved like her son. David was big for his age, both in height and girth. He didn't speak a word unless directly asked a question, and even then his answers consisted of a single word, or a nod or shake of the head if that would suffice.

Xander couldn't help but think of that morning's conversation with his mother when he looked at David. He understood why someone would choose to be quiet, but David's behavior and his dark, slowly swirling energy cloud showed no signs of joy in his life. Xander wondered what would make a person feel so bad and why a person would choose to remain so. He decided to try to speak with David if an opportunity presented itself.

After ten minutes or so of the adults asking Chrissy a barrage of questions so they could provide her with their answers, the kids took the initiative to wander off on their own, mostly in groups of twos and threes, except for Xander and David, who each walked off by himself.

Xander brought a book and elected to sit with a view of the grassy areas, the flowers and shrubs around the walkway, the pond, and most of the trees. He leaned against the trunk of a large tree with his book in his lap, taking in the beauty of the landscape. The group had met at this park before, and it was one of his favorites due to the diversity of the scenery. After a few minutes, he opened his book and started reading. It was a poetry compilation that he had been reading on and off for a couple of weeks. He liked the fact that he could read a poem or two in between novels and his nonfiction choices, and then stop at any time without having to keep track of where he was in the book. Also, he enjoyed reading the poems and trying to interpret the ideas the authors described without naming.

After reading a couple of nature poems, he closed the book and scanned the panorama. He noticed that the parents had not moved and were still talking, and he heard a high-pitched squeal from one of them a couple of times when someone from the group said something funny. He then looked around to find the other kids from the group. Most were playing a game with a disc, and a few were hiding behind trees and bushes from another who was trying to find and tag them. Then he caught sight of David, who was trudging along the walk with his head down and his hands in the pockets of his oversized coat, despite the fact that the weather was warm.

Xander looked back to the adults and, one by one, focused on their energy clouds. He noticed and compared the different color combinations, sizes, and shapes, and then reached out with his senses to feel each of them. By practicing this activity, he was able to feel and identify the variations of the clouds. Once he was finished scanning the adults' clouds, he moved on to the kids'. No two clouds were identical, and they were all interesting to

Xander. He made mental notes to distinguish any patterns between colors and sizes and shapes.

He looked at David's last, just as David himself was nearing the part of the walkway nearest to where Xander was sitting. Xander was fascinated by David's cloud. It didn't just look dark, with grays and dark oranges and black; it appeared to have a rough, scratchy texture. It reminded Xander of the ceiling in the apartment where he and his mother lived. He had heard his aunt Rebecca refer to it to his mother as "a cheap popcorn ceiling." When Xander reached out with his senses to feel it, a chill ran down his spine. It felt disgusting to him. Xander was sure that if it had a smell, it would smell like rotting garbage. He wondered what was going on with David to create such a cloud. He wanted to understand, so when David was just about to walk directly in front of him, Xander spoke up.

"Wanna sit?"

David replied without even turning his head. "No, thanks," he mumbled, barely louder than a whisper.

Xander just watched him walk on, surrounded by his gross, dirty cloud. He knew sadness was part of it, deep sadness, but from what he couldn't imagine. His thoughts drifted back to this morning's conversation again.

Why would someone choose to feel that bad? Even if bad things had happened to him, they weren't happening at the moment, so why not choose to feel good now? Xander just couldn't fathom the answer. Rather than allow himself to become frustrated from curiosity, he shifted his focus back to the beauty of the park, to his poetry, and to feeling happy.

CHAPTER 14

DAVID'S mother started bringing him to the group's outings on a regular basis. Xander had overheard her tell the other parents that, even though he would prefer to barricade himself in his room save for the far-too-seldom trips to the kitchen, she thought even the minimal social interaction he had during the meet-ups were good for him. The other parents validated the benefits the group participation would do for David, despite the fact that he had yet to interact with anyone except with his one-word mumbled responses, and then, only when he was asked a direct question.

Xander and David had not spoken since their first and only few words together, and it wasn't until a half dozen more meet-ups that they had what qualified as an actual conversation. One particular meet-up happened at an athletics park, complete with a running track, and courts and fields for a wide variety of sports. It being late morning on a weekday, the park was only being used by a few people who had unique daily routines or the flexibility to not be at work or school at that time. The parents stationed themselves at the only area in the park designed for a static activity, a small grassy area with several picnic tables. The oasis was centrally located, so the parents could drink their coffees and homemade concoctions from thermoses while still being able to periodically turn their heads to locate their children.

Xander was sitting cross-legged on the ground near the wall in a vacant handball court watching a line of ants. He faced himself directly toward the wall, partially to marvel at the ants being ants and partially so he would not have a direct view of anyone else. He did this so he could practice feeling the energy clouds of the others without looking. Before he sat down, he had scanned the clouds and associated them with the different members of the group. As he sat and slowly placed tiny obstacles in the paths of the ant line, he reached out with his senses to feel the various clouds. After a little while practicing and glancing over his shoulder to confirm, he could tell who was where in the park without even looking. He wasn't startled by David walking up behind him, as he could sense the heavy, dirt-laden energy cloud approaching. But he was startled when David spoke to him.

"What are you doing to them?

Xander turned his head to David, squinting at the sunrays, and was overwhelmed by the sight and feeling of the thick, heavy, dirty cloud encompassing him. Xander regained his composure quickly and turned back to the ants.

"Just watching them mostly. Sometimes I put something in their way to see what they'll do. I like how they don't take any time to decide. They just turn or climb, and keep moving."

David stared not at Xander, but at the line of ants veering around a couple of twigs Xander had placed perpendicular to the wall. He suddenly turned to continue his walk around the park.

Without looking up, Xander asked, "Wanna sit?"

"No, thanks," David mumbled without looking back or even lifting his head, which was bowed toward the sidewalk as usual.

Although he could feel it, Xander turned to watch David's cloud as it floated around him and away from where Xander was sitting. He wondered why David's cloud never seemed to change much in general substance or appearance like everyone else's did. He also wondered what must be going on inside of David to create and sustain that level of unhealthiness and why he didn't seem to want to talk to anyone. Xander caught the irony of his thought as soon as he thought it. He himself didn't need or want to talk to anyone either. Yet his own cloud was a very different color and did change at times, at least to some degree. He concluded that David must think differently than most people, too, but perhaps in an opposite extreme as Xander.

"Xander, time to go," Tracy yelled, waving.

Xander thought they'd be staying longer, but one look at his mother's cloud told him she wasn't feeling well. Now that he thought about it, she had been looking extra tired lately, though he couldn't understand why. She actually seemed to be taking it easy lately compared to her regular daily routine. He reached out to sense it and confirmed that the normal swirls were speckled with some irregularities.

"Are you okay?" he asked her as he approached.

Tracy produced a slight smile for Xander. "I'm fine, honey. Just tired."

They packed up their snacks and drinks, said goodbye to the group, and headed to the car. Xander caught sight of David as they backed out of the parking space. He was still walking the path, very slowly and with his hands in his coat pockets, but his head was not in its usual bowed position. It was up and pointed directly at Xander.

Xander didn't usually dwell on things. He either figured them out right away or forgot about them until he encountered them again. For some reason, however, something about this nagged at him. To satisfy his own curiosity about what made David's cloud so different from all others he had seen, he decided to do something rather novel, at least to Xander. He would make a conscious effort to get to know David.

CHAPTER

D AVID and his mother did not attend another group meet-up for almost a month. When he did, Xander was surprised to see that David's energy cloud was even darker, dingier, and barely moving. It looked to Xander like a thick, dark, sticky swamp. He felt as if David was stuck in it, and if he were to be near it for too long, that he might become stuck, too.

That's silly, Xander thought. *It can't be contagious, can it?*

He remembered the incident in the home-schooling group when Steve bullied him. Xander had pushed his own cloud into Steve's, and it did seem to have an impact. Using that experience, Xander thought it was possible for David's cloud to affect his own. With that in mind, Xander went off by himself to the opposite side of the park they were visiting that day. He sat down and leaned against a tree, closed his eyes, and imagined charging his own cloud so he would be able to be near David without being affected by the negative swamp surrounding him.

Xander had never done this before, and he didn't even know where he got the idea from or whether it would work. That didn't bother him, as many of his ideas just came to him, and rather than resist, he just followed his intuition.

He started by visualizing pure energy, which he imagined was white, rushing into his body from all around him. He visualized it filling him up, brightening his cloud so that it vibrated with power. He convinced himself the new energy renewed and enhanced his health and strength. He took some slow, deep breaths, and allowed his whole body to relax. Only then did he smile, open his eyes, and look around for David. He consciously chose not to reach out for David's cloud with his senses, knowing full well he would feel it soon enough.

He spotted David practicing his usual lumber along the sidewalk, although even more slowly than usual. He looked to Xander like he was in a trance. Not wanting to think too much about anything, Xander stood up and walked across the grass to intercept David.

David's eyes moved enough for Xander to know David saw him approaching, but David didn't respond in any other way. In light of Xander's previous attempts, he thought it best to change his strategy.

"Mind if I walk with you?"

Xander heard a barely audible or recognizable "I don't care" and fell in pace next to David.

Not wanting to hurt his chances of talking with David, Xander remained silent and just walked alongside him for a few minutes. Using only his peripheral vision, he could tell David turned his head a couple of times to look at him, but since he didn't say anything, Xander wasn't sure whether to say anything either.

David stopped suddenly and looked up and over to where the parents were, a disheveled grassy area littered with blankets, coolers, and lawn chairs. Xander followed David's gaze and then looked back at David. Xander really noticed the five inches or so in height that David had on him, but saw that his face looked just as young as, if not younger than, Xander's. His expression was unreadable, but his long stare at his mom spoke volumes of negative emotion. Without a word, David performed an about-face away from Xander and started walking back the way they had come. Xander didn't hesitate and did the same.

After a few seconds, Xander decided to say something, but he didn't want to assume or guess.

"Is something wrong?"

David scoffed under his breath, but plenty loud for Xander to hear. "Everything."

Not wanting to lose momentum, Xander followed up. "Everything? Like what?"

"Name it. Home. School. People. It's all wrong." His voice was already deep enough to make him sound like an adult to Xander.

"That sucks." Xander couldn't think of anything else to say. As they continued their walk, Xander tried to think what else there was to say to someone who thought their whole life was wrong, but couldn't think of anything. At least not anything helpful. They walked in silence until it was time for them to leave. Xander helped his mother repack the cooler and fold the blanket. As he collapsed a lawn chair, he glanced up just in time to see David and Chrissy toting their things past them to the parking lot.

"See you, Xander."

"Bye, David." Xander said. He had not even known that David had remembered his name. He called after him, "See you next time."

David looked back over his shoulder as he walked, but didn't answer. As Xander and Tracy were loading the things in the back of their small SUV, he watched David and his swampy cloud disappear into his own car. Although he did not feel like he was too affected by David's cloud, he did feel different—a bit drained from being in close proximity to the swamp-like energy. He felt glad he had charged his own cloud before the encounter and did his best not to wonder what would have happened had he not. Just thinking about it seemed to make any happiness evaporate. A distraction was needed.

"Could we stop for ice cream?" he asked as he snapped his seat belt in place.

"Ice cream? Hmmm." Tracy had put the car in reverse, but kept it in place as she considered Xander's request.

She looked him over. Although he had his usual expressionless face, she knew her son and could tell he needed the extra excursion for some reason. She had always been one to believe in a mother's intuition.

"It has been a while since we've splurged, hasn't it? Sure, let's do it." She smiled and backed out, and even Xander grinned.

CHAPTER

TRACY drove to the only remaining chain ice cream store in the city so they could indulge themselves. After waiting in the short line, they browsed through the glass cases at the variety of flavors to make their selections. Tracy chose a small sugar cone with butter pecan, and Xander opted for a cup of dark chocolate ice cream that had a fancy name because it also contained almond slivers and marshmallows. They sat in hard plastic chairs at a two-person table near a window perpendicular to and opposite the door. Xander was amused that the store only provided thin, plastic spoons. He had already broken one on his first attempt to excavate the frozen dessert from the cup.

They ate their treats in silence and were nearly finished when Tracy's cone leaked a couple drops from the bottom onto the table. They both looked quickly at the napkin dispenser to find the side closest to them empty. Tracy was sucking on the bottom of her cone as she spun the dispenser around, only to discover the other side was also empty.

"Honey, would you…" she began while leaning over the table while chewing a bit of cone and plugging the bottom of her cone with her thumb. But she didn't have to finish her sentence; Xander was already standing up and moving to get more napkins.

The adjacent tables were all occupied, so he started toward the counter that held the extra napkins, straws, and thin, plastic spoons. As he reached the counter, he experienced a feeling of déjà vu along with a sort of tickle in his energy cloud just as the door chime sounded.

Xander turned his head toward the feeling and the door while he plucked several napkins from the dispenser. He froze in place. His eyes and internal senses locked on to the shorter of the two people who had just entered, a girl about his age with long, wavy blonde hair and surrounded by a very blue, slowly swirling energy cloud.

He set himself in motion again and turned back to his mother without taking his eyes off of the girl who, from the moment she had entered, was staring straight back at Xander. She was smiling the same, beautiful smile Xander remembered, and he gawked at her all the way back to his seat.

"She sure is pretty," Tracy said as she took the napkins.

Xander finally broke eye contact with the girl, who had just reached the front counter with the tall, sandy blond-haired man who was likely her father.

"Yeah," replied Xander, trying his best to sound disinterested.

He knew his mother did not remember the girl from the pool all those years ago, but he had never forgotten her. Her and her magnificent blue energy cloud. He scraped his ice cream cup and ate the last bite, then nonchalantly turned his head toward the front counter. Her father's cloud, filled with blues and greens vibrating and swirling rather quickly, seemed dwarfed by the girl's own cloud. Xander thought hers moved so slowly and gracefully that it looked almost as if it were dancing. He could not get over just how blue her cloud was… and not just most of it—the entire cloud was the same true blue. He lowered his gaze and realized she was staring back at him again. No, above him. She shifted her own eyes down and locked on to Xander's. She smiled. He wondered whether she remembered him. She turned back to the front, responding to her father's elbow nudge.

"Ready, Romeo?" Tracy teased.

"Sure." Xander grabbed the used napkins and stuffed them into his cup, then stood up and headed for the door with his mother.

He deposited the remnants of their visit into the trash container and pushed the door open, allowing his mother to exit first. As she passed him, he looked back to the counter. The girl was smiling at him, and with the sunlight from outside behind him, he was able to see the beautiful light brown of her eyes. She waved a small, discreet wave to him which he returned before walking out. He could still feel her energy cloud even as he buckled his seat belt. He felt warmth and peace coming from her cloud, like he was being hugged… and he did his very best to hug her back.

CHAPTER

Tracy was already tired of making excuses. First she had asked Rebecca to come over and keep an eye on Xander while she attended a networking function where she might be able to pick up some more virtual work projects, and now she had asked Chrissy if she would please drive Xander to today's unschool meet-up. Both were lies. Both times she had gone to the medical clinic. The first time was to have a doctor examine her and, she hoped, explain why she had been experiencing headaches, low-grade fevers, and rashes. She had put off making an appointment until the frequency of the symptoms had increased and when she discovered an unexplained lump near her armpit. Her second clinic visit was to obtain the results from the barrage of tests the doctor had ordered. Luckily, she had been able to have all of the tests performed during the first visit and didn't have to lie a third time.

When her name was called, she followed a young woman past the reception desk, through a door, and down a short hallway to a room like the one she had visited for the exam. The nurse asked her to have a seat and said that the doctor would be with her shortly. Tracy sat down in a chair next to a suspended computer terminal and a stool that was obviously for the staff. She was thinking that the term *shortly* had a different definition in the medical community than it did in the rest of the world when the same doctor who had ordered the tests for her, Dr. Stattler, walked into the room.

"Good afternoon, Ms. Noxx," Dr. Stattler said, shaking her hand and pulling the stool under him to sit.

He smiled, though it was obvious it was only a partial, polite smile. He looked to be nearing fifty, with traces of gray just starting to appear at his temples, and Tracy found herself mildly attracted to him. It was hard for her to gauge his personality since, at least during her one previous encounter with him, he was serious and friendly, but in a professional manner only.

"Hello, Doctor Stattler," she began. "So, what's what?" She scrutinized his face and thought she caught the smallest look of concern despite his smile. She was suddenly nervous, but told herself she was being silly.

Dr. Stattler turned the chart onto his lap, adjusted his stool, and looked Tracy in the eyes for a second before he spoke. Tracy felt gooseflesh on her arms as she watched his smile disappear.

"Ms. Noxx… I ordered a biopsy at your last visit, hoping the results would force me to disregard my original suspicion. Unfortunately, the results confirmed a diagnosis. You have non-Hodgkin's lymphoma."

An immediate, icy numbness came over Tracy. The doctor, having experience in delivering similar, shocking news, understood her paralysis and waited for a minute before continuing.

"We'll have to run some more tests, of course, to determine what stage your cancer has reached, and then we can decide on the best course of action with regard to treatment."

Cancer. I have cancer, Tracy told herself.

She dropped her head and stared at the ground between their feet. The surreal feeling easily overpowered her confusion and helped her maintain her composure. That and the shock of the life-changing information she had just received. As the mental frost started to thaw, her thoughts went to Xander.

She wondered what would happen to him if she were no longer able to care for him and asked herself, *Who else understands him?*

She hated the thought of him having to live with her sister. Rebecca would have him back in public school in a heartbeat and, in all probability, she'd also have him seeing a shrink and taking medication. She thought that he would have a choice because of his age, but his choices would be limited. Her mind was finally beginning to connect with the present and with her body, and tears started to well. She couldn't stand the thought of

Xander living with someone other than family, but she couldn't think of what other options he would have.

"Ms. Noxx?"

Dr. Stattler's voice and his hand on her shoulder interrupted her internal monologue.

"We have trained professionals you can talk with that can help you deal with the... nonmedical challenges, but you should also talk to someone you know. Do you have family or a friend you can talk to?"

"Yes." Tracy sniffed, restraining the urge to cry. "Yes, I do."

"That's good." He turned the chart back over and started writing. "I'm going to order the tests you will need, and they need to be done quickly so we know how to treat this. Every day we wait can make a difference, so you'll need to be on call for whenever we can get you in, okay?"

Tracy nodded and sniffed some more.

The stool slid backward as the doctor stood in place.

"This is treatable, Ms. Noxx. It's not quite as curable as Hodgkin's, but you can beat it."

Tracy nodded and did her best to produce some semblance of a smile. "Thank you, doctor."

He left, and a few minutes later, a friendly nurse came back in with a tissue box and a cup of water. The nurse also gave her a list with scheduled appointments for her tests and went over the specific pretest instructions for a couple of them. Tracy thanked him without looking at the list, took a couple of tissues, and left.

She sat crying in her car for minutes that seemed to last for hours. The windows were fogged from her sweat due to the warm temperature, but also from her breath as she bawled out of fear and anger. At last she was able to swallow properly and stop her crying. Her expression changed from a look of contorted pain to one of pure determination.

"Xander won't have to make a choice," she said aloud. "I *will* beat this."

As she started the car and headed home, she thought silently to herself, *or literally die trying.*

CHAPTER 18

TRACY'S ruse did not fool Xander when she told him Chrissy would be driving him to the next meet-up. Although he wasn't a hundred percent certain what she was doing, he guessed correctly that she was going to see a doctor. Aside from the increasingly frequent headaches she had been having and the recent appearance of strange rashes on her arms and neck, he had also noticed an unusual pattern steadily growing in her energy cloud. What was once a few tan speckles had eventually manifested into a solid tan swirl of its own, though darker than the first speckles, that was weaving itself around the other colors. Xander had long since learned that shades of brown or black were not good and often were a sign of being unhealthy or of disease.

Since he had learned how to start feeling the clouds, he could usually sense when someone was sick without even looking at them or at their cloud. Some of his past experiences had taught him that clouds could influence other clouds, so he did his best not to spend too much time around the clouds with toxic colors. He hadn't worried too much about his mother up to now, since the colors could mean something as simple as a cold or the flu. It all depended on the shade, amount, and movement of the unhealthy color. Now, however, he was starting to worry.

Chrissy and David pulled up to the curb in an older red minivan, and Chrissy honked the horn. Tracy peeked out the window to confirm it was them and then walked Xander out to the car. Xander slid open the side door, sat in the short bench seat, and fastened his seat belt, placing his lunch on the floor in front of him. Tracy walked up to the passenger door and bent over enough to be able to see Chrissy as well as David.

"Good morning!" she said to Chrissy with a smile. "Hi, David."

When Tracy touched his shoulder as part of her greeting, David recoiled enough for everyone to notice. Tracy's smile shortened as she retracted her hand and placed it on the door frame next to her other hand.

"Thank you so much for driving Xander. I really hate to impose on you, but this conference is such a great opportunity." The lie tasted sour in her mouth.

"No problem whatsoever. We're going anyway, and your place is really not that far out of the way. Beautiful neighborhood, by the way," Chrissy said with a smile.

"Oh, thanks," Tracy replied as she made an obligatory sweep of her head up and down the street. "So, I probably won't be back until at least 4:30, if that's okay."

"Don't worry about it. Just text when you're home and I'll drop him off."

"Bye, honey, love you," Tracy said to Xander as she stood up. Xander smiled and raised his hand in a wave, and off they went.

Chrissy did most of the talking during the forty-minute drive to the park. Occasionally, she would ask Xander a question, but only, it seemed, to give herself another prompt to continue talking. Xander did not mind answering her questions, and she didn't seem to mind his concise responses. He did notice that she didn't speak to David nor he to either of them for the entire ride. His mother would talk about him every once in a while, but what may have started out as a funny anecdote or even a compliment would end in criticism.

David had raised the window and stared through it the entire trip, looking at nothing in particular. His energy cloud was now a churning, sticky brown puddle. It reminded Xander of the contents of a witch's cauldron in a movie he had seen once. Xander felt greasy, like the filthy, slimy ooze in the cloud was rubbing up against him. He practically sprung from the van as soon as they parked.

Chrissy accepted Xander's offer to help tote things, since she brought an oversized cooler with ice and extra drinks to share.

"That's so sweet. Thank you, Xander."

He placed his own lunch in the cooler, and then he and David each lent an arm to carry it to the field where the group was initially meeting.

There were no new people to introduce, so the kids were able to disperse almost right away. At once, David started walking toward the perimeter of the park, and Xander followed. At first, he trailed behind him a few yards, wanting to keep some distance from David's cloud, though he could feel it anyway. Then he remembered that he could charge his own energy cloud and thought it best to do that before getting any closer… just in case.

He thought back to how he had done it before and started visualizing his body receiving and being filled by a surge of bright, white energy from all around. This time, he received a different nudge to also picture bright and vibrant green energy shooting into him from the Earth. The green energy was absorbed by and enhanced the pure, white energy. Once he imagined his body saturated with new, strong, healthy energy, he quickened his strides until he was walking side by side with David, matching his pace.

Xander was being conscious of David's cloud and whether it was having an impact on his own, and he wasn't sure how to begin a conversation, so they meandered around the park for a while in silence. The sky was unusually gray and seemed to Xander to join forces with David's energy. Xander felt like his own cloud was being compressed like the cans in a trash compactor. He had seen a compactor in action during one of the unschooling trips and thought hydraulic power was interesting, but he was more impressed with watching the sheer force at work on the various types of metal cans that were being contorted beneath the press. Xander did not enjoy the feeling and decided to start talking, both to learn more about David and to distract himself from the sensation of being flattened.

"I can see stuff… energy… around people. Animals, too. Technically, they're called auras, but I think of them as energy clouds." Xander paused, wondering why he was telling this to David, especially since he had never even told his mother about being able to see the clouds. "I've been able to see them for years." He stopped there, waiting to see if David would react to his sharing.

Xander glanced sideways at David's face and saw it had changed. Hoping the new expression meant that David was listening and interested, Xander added, "I see yours."

David stopped walking and made eye contact with Xander for the first time. "What does it look like?"

Xander looked up at David's baby face and into eyes so bright blue he was surprised he had not noticed their striking color before. Although he never considered lying, Xander thought giving David a detailed description of his cloud would probably not help at this time.

"It looks kind of dark and... unhealthy," he answered honestly.

"It figures," David said and then resumed walking.

Xander walked alongside again, unsure of how to proceed. He wanted to help David feel better, but he could never understand why people chose to feel bad when they could choose to feel good.

"When I find myself feeling bad..." but David stopped to look at him again and cut him off.

"Look, I know you want to help. Everybody wants to help, but you can't. You just can't. You don't understand my life." He started walking again.

Xander started to follow, but David added, "I want to be alone right now. It's not worth it," stopping Xander in his tracks.

Xander called after him, "What's not worth it?"

"Life."

It seemed so obvious to Xander, but he thought maybe if he explained to David how he always has the choice to feel good then, with practice, he would be able to see that choice before him in any given situation and act on it. It now appeared to Xander, however, that David either did not want to feel good or didn't know he was capable of choosing to feel good.

Xander had more than one epiphany while standing on the sidewalk, staring at David walking away on that afternoon. The first was that he was able to see things differently than anyone he had ever met. Maybe it was because he could see and sense the energy around him, but he knew it was more than that. His mind worked differently. Not necessarily better, but differently. The second epiphany was that, because everyone thought differently, he couldn't expect others to understand everything that he did.

He had a third epiphany on the sidewalk under the gray sky that day. Whether or not it made sense to Xander, despite the choice everyone had to feel good, some people just chose not to.

That last epiphany was validated the very next day. He had finished breakfast and headed back to his bedroom to read when he heard his mom answer her cellphone. He felt the sudden change in her energy cloud before he heard the alarm in her voice. He placed his book down in his lap and waited for his mother to appear at his bedroom door. She had tears in her eyes as she came into the room and sat down next to him, taking his hands in hers.

"That was Chrissy," she said, sniffing.

"She's at the hospital with David. He tried to kill himself."

CHAPTER 19

Tracy sat at the kitchen table and stared at the small patio through the sliding glass door as she cradled her tea cup with both hands, savoring the warmth. She had planned on sitting Xander down and breaking the news about her cancer to him the day after her diagnosis, but she couldn't find it in herself to give her son tragic news twice on the same day. This was despite the fact that he had not reacted when she told him about David, at least not in any way she could detect. Of course, that was not unusual for Xander.

She thought back to his earlier childhood, trying to remember how he had responded in the past to traumatic events. But she knew she would not be able to recall any significant reactions, because there were none. She had witnessed him laugh often, cry a few times when he had been physically hurt, and get mad... well, never. The times he would cry when he was a baby were out of frustration and meant to communicate his hunger or discomfort, but even then it didn't seem like he was truly upset. He would always stop crying as soon as she realized what he was trying to convey. She had to struggle to even remember two times when she had even expected an emotional reaction from Xander.

The first was when they had been rear-ended while driving downtown. They hadn't been going too fast, but the impact had been hard enough to jar them both and to do noticeable damage to both vehicles. Xander was only five at the time, and Tracy was glad he was still plenty small enough to be riding in a car seat. After a few seconds, when her disorientation had left, she looked back to him in a panic, only to find him swinging his little legs and staring back at her as if nothing had happened. Tracy had broken down and cried out of fear and anger, but Xander seemed just fine.

The second time she had expected him to react was when he was seven and she told him her mother had passed away. Before she died, her mother had visited them often, sometimes accompanied by Rebecca and sometimes on her own. She would sit him on her lap on the couch and read to him or let him play with the pages. He was always very comfortable with her and allowed her to hug and kiss him as much as she liked without pulling away. He hadn't cried or appeared sad when she told him Grandma went to heaven, but Tracy thought he might just not understand. She thought things would be different when he saw her at the open-casket funeral, but they weren't, save for Xander looking above and all around the casket as if something were missing.

No, Xander just didn't react to things, at least not outwardly. Now that he was old enough to communicate, Tracy could talk with him, but his understanding of the world and of people was unique. It was not fair to assume he didn't have feelings or empathy. It was just that he did not always look like he had feelings. He didn't look like she or other people expected him to look at times. Tracy wondered how he would feel when she told him she was dying. She wondered how he would feel, if he would feel anything, and if he would react to the news. Most of all, she wondered which she feared most—the potential grief her son would experience when he learned about her imminent death, or the real or perceived absence of it.

Tracy decided she would give Xander the benefit of the doubt that he was upset about David somewhere below the surface. She would not tell him about her cancer yet. She would wait a couple of days… or maybe a week before troubling him with more bad news.

Of course, knowing Xander like she did, it wouldn't shock her if he already suspected something was wrong with her. He had always had a sense of how she was feeling, especially when she was feeling sick or sad, and now she was both. The more she thought about that, the more certain she was that Xander already knew something. He probably didn't know it was cancer, but she was sure he would know she was not well. And she was right.

CHAPTER 20

THE next unschooling meet-up was anything but normal for the group, even considering how weird unschooling itself was when compared to the more conventional methods of educating children. Instead of meeting at one of the many beautiful parks to enjoy the weather and nature, they all gathered at the home of the founders of the group, Robert and Bonnie Simms. The couple had started the group for their three children almost five years ago. They attended the group activities together at first, but then Robert accepted a promotion and started working from the corporate office.

The Simms had strongly suggested that they all meet to openly discuss the impact of David's suicide attempt on the individual group members. They thought it would be a therapeutic experience to allow everyone, especially the children, to share their feelings. Sitting together and talking to one another in a central area was routine for the parents, but the kids were used to being off on their own and were having a hard time sitting still, let alone dealing with the awkward situation.

The sofas and matching recliners were turned toward the center of the room, and chairs from other parts of the house filled in spaces between to form some semblance of a circle. Xander looked around the large living room from the leather padded dining chair where he had landed. He understood the intent of the gathering, but didn't think it was necessary since none of the other families were close with David. Xander had spent more time with David than anyone in the group, save for David's mother, but he didn't know why they would think the minimal contact and interaction he had had with David would warrant an emotional support group. In any case, he would be able to practice shielding and projecting his energy.

Enough people showed up that the Simms exhausted the chair inventory from their dining room and home office to accommodate everyone. In total, there were fifteen in attendance, the Simms and five pairs of parent and child, more than what usually attended the weekly meet-ups. Xander recognized everyone, even though he had seen two of the kids only once or twice in his time in the group. He watched them, some fidgeting and some staring anywhere but toward the other members. Not one of them seemed to want to be there, and all wanted it to end quickly, but no one wanted to be the one to start talking.

Xander became bored with waiting and began examining the energy clouds of the people sitting around him. Although he saw a wide variety of color combinations, shapes, and movements of the clouds, none of them stood out to him. He was wondering, once again, why they had decided to meet like this when Bonnie Simms stood up and began talking.

"Welcome and thank you all for coming."

Xander felt relief from every energy cloud in the room that the process had finally started.

"As you have heard, David Carlson tried to take his life recently. His mother, Chrissy, understandably is not present, but has asked me to convey her gratitude for cards and prayers for David and their family."

Xander watched the parents look around at each other, their faces either taking credit or showing gratitude or guilt. Tracy and Xander were one of the families that had sent a card. They took a while picking out the card because they didn't think a sympathy card or a get-well card was appropriate. Finally, they found one that had a beautiful landscape on the front and was blank on the inside. Tracy had penned, *Our thoughts and prayers are with you,* and signed her name. Xander wrote, *Hope to see you soon,* and answered his mother's puzzled look by telling her they didn't actually pray for him.

Another boy who was present, Troy, raised his hand.

"Yes, Troy?" Bonnie asked.

Troy dropped his head a little, but kept his eyes on Bonnie. "What did he do?"

Bonnie swallowed, then rubbed her hands together as she responded. "He swallowed some pills."

Xander watched Troy's and several other clouds simultaneously slow down momentarily, and he guessed that they were adding the new details to their mental picture of the event.

Bonnie took advantage of the continuing silence to ask, "Now, who has anything they would like to share? Don't be shy. You can feel safe to say anything."

She looked around the circle at each face, one by one, and stopped at Xander's.

"Xander? What about you? You were closest with David... do you have anything you'd like to share?"

Of course, everyone else gladly looked toward Xander, since they were relieved of any pressure to speak at the moment. Xander, on the other hand, was at a loss. He assumed by the question being posed directly to him, as well as by everyone intently staring at him, that he was supposed to say something meaningful, but he didn't know what to say. More than that, he didn't think there was anything for him to say, and since he wasn't one for speaking unnecessarily, he simply said it.

"I don't have anything to say."

There was some uncomfortable stirring around the room, but Bonnie's eyes never left Xander's.

She smiled a sympathetic smile and said, "Well, just tell us how you feel about your friend trying to... to hurt himself."

Hurt himself? I thought he tried to kill himself. Xander didn't understand why Bonnie couldn't just say it. *Isn't that the reason we're all sitting around in your living room right now?* He realized he had an audience awaiting his reply, but again, he could only think to say the obvious truth.

"He didn't just try to hurt himself, he tried to kill himself. I wish he didn't, but I don't live his life. I assume he must have had a good reason for doing that... at least in his mind," he said.

Xander heard air being sucked past teeth from different people in the circle and looked around at the various expressions in the group. Some looked appalled and some wore various other looks of disapproval.

"There is no good reason to kill yourself," Bonnie served back.

"Not to you maybe, but to David there was," Xander answered.

Tracy put her hand on Xander's leg in an attempt to both support him and stop him from being what she was sure others thought of as insensitive or cold. She knew he was not intending to argue or be defensive, but Bonnie and many others did not know Xander like she did and, even if they did, may not understand him.

Bonnie was visibly agitated. The other group members watched her as she paused, closed her eyes, inhaled deeply through her nose, and then exhaled through her mouth before opening her eyes.

She smiled and glared at Xander, and then looked around the room and said, "Okay, who's next?"

Xander could tell by her body language and by the reddish tint to Bonnie's cloud that she was irritated, and he knew why. His answers had not met her expectations. He could tell that some of the others in the room were also not pleased with what he had said. This type of reaction by people never failed to strike Xander as odd. He knew it was not acceptable to lie, but he also knew that if the truth he spoke was not something other people understood, they would become angry or frustrated. He decided not to dwell on the matter, since he knew from experience he had no control over what people thought or believed. Also, he had other things on his mind, like his mother and whatever was wrong with her… and her energy cloud.

The drive home was quiet, but not because either Tracy or Xander were emotional about the group discussion or even about David. Although they did not know it, they were both thinking about Tracy's health… or lack thereof.

On the way, Xander reached out with his senses to his mother's cloud. He pictured his own cloud forming a finger-like shape and poking into her cloud. He could not understand what exactly he was experiencing, except that it was not pleasant. He immediately felt ill, but the feeling was somewhat distant. He tried to explain it to himself by imagining it was like playing in the mud with gloves on—his skin might not actually come in contact with the mud, but it would still feel sticky and slimy.

He made his cloud retreat and he looked at his mother. Even if he could not see or feel the wrongness of the coffee color weaving itself through her cloud, he would know something was wrong. Besides the headaches he knew she had even when she didn't complain, the red splotches on her skin were spreading and becoming more visible. She had been attempting to cover them up, but the weather was often too warm for extra clothing, and makeup only served to draw more attention. Even her faced looked different. It was still the face of his mother, but Xander thought it looked stressed and serious, and older.

"Mother, what's wrong with you?" Xander asked, continuing to look at her.

Tracy was only surprised for a second. She kept her eyes on the road and answered, "Nothing, honey—I'm fine," although she knew full well that his question meant he knew she wasn't.

"You're sick. Do you know what's wrong with you?"

Xander had always been able to tell when his mother didn't want to talk about something and, in the past, he had never minded and would either stop talking or change the subject. This time was different, and he was determined to learn the truth, whether or not she was comfortable sharing it.

Tracy's mind raced and then went blank. She recovered after a couple of seconds and she felt grateful her brain and muscle memory had kicked in enough to keep the car in the lane. She saw a shopping center just up ahead, put her blinker on, turned in, and parked in a space far from the stores. She put the car in park, turn off the ignition, and turned to look at her son. She smiled as much as she could while trying to keep from bawling, though she was unable to stop her eyes from welling and a single tear from falling down each cheek.

She laid her hand on his hair and then slid it down the side of his face, resting it on his cheek.

"Aw, honey... I have cancer."

She blinked and spilled more tears as she fought to maintain her smile. Sniffing, she began explaining what she knew about her disease to her son, emphasizing the potential of the treatment as much for her as for him.

Xander's face remained unchanged as he listened to his mother and slowly associated her words with meaning. *Not just sick. Cancer. Non-Hodgkin's lymphoma.* He would research that on his own when they got home. Other thoughts formed in his mind as certain words his mother said jumped out at him. Words like *mortality rate* and *can significantly prolong my life span.* In a manner uncommon for Xander, his imagination started working without being complemented by his rational mind. He thought of his mother… sick, weak, in pain… dying. He thought of her smile, her hugs, eating together, reading together, and laughing together. He thought about how he would miss all of those things… how he would miss her. Overwhelmed with grief, Xander experienced unusual physical sensations, at least for him. His throat swelled, he began trembling, and his own eyes filled up and spilled. He fell as a helpless heap against his mother and, for the first time in years, Xander cried.

CHAPTER 27

OVER the next couple of months, Tracy and Xander each came to grips with the reality of her cancer in their own way. Tracy did her best, which in her mind meant receiving the chemotherapy and other unnatural treatments into her body, and Xander did his best by supporting his mother despite his being able to tell by her energy cloud that the chemicals were ineffective at reducing the cancer. He was also able to see with his own eyes the unwanted side effects caused by the treatment. At times, especially right after a treatment, it proved difficult for Tracy to function normally and get herself through a routine day, but she tried anyway. She also continued to take Xander to unschooling meet-ups and activities when she was feeling well enough to drive. When she wasn't, all she had to do was ask, and one of the other parents was always happy to transport Xander.

Although Tracy would rather have not told anyone about her cancer, her struggle was obvious, and so she told the parents who regularly attended the meet-ups and, of course, she told her sister.

As Tracy expected, her interactions with the other unschooling parents were awkward at first, full of sympathetic comments and offers of prayers, ears, and shoulders for emotional support. She also was not surprised by Rebecca's reaction. When Tracy broke the news to her sister, Rebecca was shocked. She cried with and hugged Tracy for a minute and then wiped her own tears and started making a list of demands for Tracy to follow. She insisted on her having a strict diet, lots of sunshine and extra vitamins, and of course, adhering to every last bit of her oncologist's prescribed treatment regimen of chemo and medication, and even radiation if it came to that. Tracy didn't argue, and she humored her sister as much as she could.

Xander had his own challenges. He not only had to watch his mother struggle as her energy cloud became darker from the cancer, but he was able to see and feel its impact on other clouds. Despite his mother's outward attempts to stay positive, her energy cloud expanded into any other nearby cloud, including his own. He saw and felt that when her cloud would come in contact with another, the colors in the other cloud would dim. First it would only look subdued along the edges, but the longer his mother's cloud was touching, the more the dullness would spread, slowly seeping into the other cloud in all directions. When Xander first observed that happen in other people, he saw changes in them. Some people would start to feel tired and other would suddenly not feel well. He even noticed a difference in people who were sympathetic and those who were empathetic, with the former showing more signs of being impacted than the latter. The changes Xander saw were usually subtle, but they were there.

As soon as he realized that, he developed a habit of charging his energy every morning when he woke and again at night just before he went to sleep. He knew he couldn't catch his mother's cancer, but the more saturated her cloud became with the coffee-colored swirls, which were growing in size and density, the more he felt its effects.

On the morning of one of the scheduled meet-up days, Xander heard his mother vomiting as he passed the bathroom on the way to the kitchen. Before he made his breakfast, he grabbed the unschooling group contact list from beneath a magnet on the refrigerator to call and ask one of the parents who regularly attended for a ride to the meet-up. He decided to ask Mrs. Jarvis. As far as Xander knew, she and her nine-year-old daughter, Heather, had never missed a meet-up or an activity since he had joined the group. Plus, she had given him a ride previously and had remarked to his mother that they lived pretty close to one another.

"Hi, Tracy," Mrs. Jarvis answered.

She has our home phone number in her contact list, Xander assumed.

"It's Xander, Mrs. Jarvis."

"Oh, hello, Xander. Is everything all right?"

"Yeah. My mother is just not feeling too well this morning, and I was wondering if you wouldn't mind giving me a ride today."

"Of course I don't mind! Tell your mom I'm happy to take you anytime. I'll be by about 11:15 to pick you up, okay?"

"I'll be ready. Thank you, Mrs. Jarvis."

Xander hung up the phone and turned to see his mother leaning against the wall in the hallway entrance to the kitchen. "Thank you so much, honey. This nausea's just kicking my butt." She walked over and hugged Xander, resting her head on his.

"I'm gonna go back to bed for a bit. Can you pack a lunch for yourself?"

"Sure," answered Xander, returning her hug while recharging his energy cloud.

Tracy released him and headed back down the hallway, saying over her shoulder, "Please remember to lock the door when you leave."

"I will."

When Mrs. Jarvis pulled up to the curb and beeped the horn, Xander was ready, as he had been watching for her out the window. He jumped up, grabbed his lunch from the counter, and headed out, pulling the door shut extra hard in case his mother was listening for it. He climbed into the passenger seat, said good morning to Mrs. Jarvis and Heather, and they headed to the park.

The weather was unseasonably cool, but the sun was warm enough to deter outerwear. Xander appreciated not sweating as he walked laps around the park until he decided on a comfortable-looking tree trunk. He always tried to sit where he would have a panoramic view of the park and still see the adults catching up on their latest stories and sharing snacks. He sat down against a tree that was leaning away from the center of the park, and so he was able to recline a bit. Removing his shoes and socks and setting them to the side of the tree, he allowed his bare feet to come in contact with the soft, cool ground while he ran his hands back and forth through the thick grass.

He recharged himself, imagining his body receiving a surge of pure white energy from all around him while a vibrant green energy coming up from the earth also filled him. He believed that by removing his shoes and socks and touching the ground with his bare hands and feet, the energy from the earth could flow more easily into him. Leaning back against the tree trunk, he closed his eyes and breathed deeply through his nose, one by one accessing each of his non-seeing senses. First, he listened, identifying what sounds he could. He could hear traffic, an airplane fading into the distance, and intermittent sounds from birds and from young children on the playground. He then focused on the earthy smells around him, though he could not identify a specific scent, and then on the lingering taste of toothpaste.

Next, he shifted his concentration to what he could physically feel. Starting from his head, he could feel the coolness of the shade and the unevenness of the tree bark on the back of his head. Slowly moving down his body, he could feel the stretch of his t-shirt, a knot pressing into his shoulder blade, the tension of his lower back muscles supporting him, and powerful energy surging up from the ground through the cool grass into his hands and feet, up his limbs and into his core. He felt rippling waves spreading back out from his center to fill every part of his body.

Feeling relaxed, Xander felt like he was vibrating outward in all directions. He had the sensation of becoming part of the tree, part of the ground, and part of the atmosphere surrounding him. Peace. That was all there was. He did not try to think, but to let himself be in that space, in that moment. To let himself just be.

A feeling stirred within him. His mind engaged, and he tried to associate that feeling with words in his head. The stillness in his mind started to slip away, faster and faster, as his consciousness returned to his body and to his empirical senses. He opened his eyes and shrugged his shoulders, stretching. Bittersweet emotion filled him for a moment, as he felt the buzz of excitement remembering the new, expanding experience, but also a tinge of disappointment at losing that feeling. He had no idea how much time had passed while his eyes were closed, so he looked toward the adults, who didn't appear to have even changed positions. Xander watched them talking and eating, when the feeling that had pulled him out of his recent experience returned. This time, however, he was able to associate that feeling with a word. *David.*

CHAPTER 22

CHRISSY and David were just getting out of their van as Xander's eyes followed his internal sense to David's energy cloud. It had changed some, but not enough to make it unfamiliar to Xander. The brown, stew-like appearance had given way to a gritty, charcoal gray that still moved as a thick, slow sludge. It reminded Xander a little of fresh poured concrete, but made from dirty, recycled cement. He couldn't help but reach out to feel it and noticed that the feel of it had also changed. Rather than a swamp of negativity, it gave Xander an unpleasant sensation of cold dampness. It wasn't quite as bad as before, but it was still bad, and Xander was glad he had just recharged his own cloud.

He watched David walk with his mother to the area where the adults were camped. They stood in place for a moment or two, and then Chrissy gave David an unreturned hug. David did not stay to help Chrissy unpack the food or chairs, but turned and walked off, ignoring the awkward silence and stares that followed him until he reached the perimeter path.

Xander watched him too. The path veered near to where he was sitting, and when he approached, David stopped and looked over at him.

"Mind if I sit?"

"Sure," Xander said, glad that he didn't react or show any signs of his surprise. He was intrigued at the changes in energy and behavior he was seeing.

David lowered himself to the ground into a cross-legged position, sitting on the bottom of his oversized coat and wrapping his arms around his knees.

"The only way my mom would let me go out is if I promised to do something social." His head was bowed, but his eyes looked at Xander. "Talking is social, right?"

"Absolutely," Xander answered with a small grin.

Xander didn't realize he was still staring until David broke off eye contact and turned his head. Xander decided to use the leverage to his advantage and start a conversation. He knew neither of them would be up for small talk, so he chose to be his normal, direct self. He also guessed that David would respond with a predictable "no" if Xander were to ask if he wanted to talk about his suicide attempt, so he tried a different approach.

"Why did you take all the pills?"

David's eyebrows lifted in mild surprise. "'Cause I wanted to kill myself," he answered.

Not to be deterred, Xander pressed on. "Why did you want to kill yourself?"

David stared at Xander, but the lack of expression on Xander's face made him unsure of any bad intentions, so he lowered his defenses and his sternness softened and disappeared. He shifted his legs so he was sitting on his hip and leaning on one arm, and he looked down and started pulling blades of grass from the ground with his other hand.

"I don't really know." He paused and rubbed some grass between his thumb and fingers. "I guess it was more that I didn't think there was anything worth living for."

He paused again and Xander looked from David to the cloud surrounding him.

"What about now?"

"There's still nothing really... apparently, I even suck at suicide."

But something's changed, Xander thought as he inspected David's cloud.

He knew the change in color and feel signified some improvement, if only a little. He tried to focus on the energy, scrutinizing it for any signs or hints of meaning for the change. He looked at the individual swirls, different shades of gray all twisting and weaving and tangling and untangling themselves in the cloud. Then something caught his eye. During the dance-like movement of the energy, he saw a tiny color variance between two separating swirls. It disappeared almost instantly, but then he noticed another, and another. At first he thought he was seeing bluish sparkles, but he quickly realized that he was seeing a light blue background color that was barely visible due to the massive amount of gray that was all but saturating David's cloud.

Without thinking about what he was doing, he reached forward with his own cloud to touch David's. Anytime he caught the color variations, he tried to push his own cloud into those spaces. He wasn't sure exactly what he was trying to do, but he was following his intuition in hopes that he could help David know the light blue energy was also present. Maybe he needed to help him balance his energy.

But it wasn't working. Every time Xander attempted to force his own energy, it would be deflected or just stopped. He had a strong impulse to relax instead of push his energy and, when he stopped forcing it, his own energy easily flowed into the openings between the gray swirls in David's cloud.

"What are you doing?"

David was staring at Xander, who realized he had been squinting in a concentrated stare above David's head as he moved his energy.

He dropped his gaze to meet David's questioning stare. He didn't think about lying, but he also didn't want to answer the question. He didn't know how David felt after talking about his energy cloud and the fact that Xander believed he could see them.

"So... if you suck at suicide, maybe you should try to find something you're good at."

"Right," David replied, returning his grass tearing. "I've tried. It's always the same. Plus... there's people around... and people suck."

"Thanks a lot," Xander said, doing his best to sound sarcastic, and he saw the tiniest smirk on David's face.

He felt a spark of hope and continued allowing his energy to touch the background color in David's cloud, but he did so solely with his internal sense. He wanted to keep his eyes on David if he could this time. Xander waited to see if David was going to continue talking. When he didn't, Xander spoke up again to keep the conversation going: "You know, I know people can be... difficult to be around."

David scoffed, but Xander continued.

"But if you keep trying things, you might eventually find something you do like, and then you can focus on the thing you're doing instead of the people. I do that last part a lot. Not for the same reason, but it works."

He paused, half expecting another defensive response, but none came. David just continued to tear grass and sprinkle the broken blades in front of him. His brow was furrowed, and Xander hoped that meant he was considering Xander's words.

They sat in silence under the tree until they heard a shrill whistle from the adults, indicating that it was time to pack up. David had spent the time thinking and excavating the ground in front of him until there was nearly a square foot of dirt visible.

Xander, pretending to watch him, focused on allowing his own energy to influence David's. Though he was not certain it wasn't his imagination, he thought some of the light blue patches between the cement in David's cloud had grown. Xander's attention was broken by the whistle, and his attention and other senses snapped into focus.

As David used his hand to rake the torn grass blades to the cover the bare dirt, Xander noticed there was still a glow over the barren space. It was different than the glow over the surrounding grassy areas, but it was visible. Xander wondered if the Earth had energy regardless of whether something was growing in it. He guessed there were roots all around, and perhaps insects and other life, too, that would have their own, tiny energy clouds surrounding them. Of course, he thought, it could be that the earth itself had its own energy, independent of its indigenous life. That must be why he imagined the green energy coming up from the ground to help charge his own.

The boys both stood, swept their pants with their hands, and started walking toward the rest of the group. Xander refocused on David's energy cloud and was pleased to find that it wasn't just his imagination. Instead of periodic sparkles of light blue between the gray swirls, there were now some plainly obvious color variations. It had worked. It even felt a bit better to Xander or, at least, not quite as drab.

They were nearing the group, but were still several yards away when Xander stopped suddenly.

"Oh…" Xander said, and David stopped and turned to face him.

"Something I've realized..." Xander started, wanting to implant what he thought was a crucial lesson he had learned about people. "... just don't wait for other people to make things better for you. Most of the time, they can't. You really have to do it yourself."

David inhaled deeply and his eyes filled with tears. He swallowed hard and gave a small nod, and they started walking again.

The ride home was pleasant. Mrs. Jarvis talked most of the time, but stopped herself just long enough to ask Heather and Xander questions that only required brief answers. As they pulled up in front of Xander's house, she put the car in park and turned toward Xander.

"That was so sweet of you to spend time with David. He really needs good friends right now."

Xander nodded but thought it was a strange thing to say. It seemed to him that David needed good friends before now.

He said his thanks and goodbyes and turned to see his mother waving thanks from the opened front door. Xander smiled at her despite being appalled by her energy cloud, which seemed to be getting darker, thicker, and slower by the week. He quickly turned his attention from the cloud and was excited to see her. Tracy could tell, and she beamed back at him. She assumed he had just missed her after being away for the day. What she didn't know was that, although he would prefer that she had been at the park with him, he wasn't thinking that he missed her. He was just really excited to practice his new energy trick... on her.

CHAPTER 23

As months passed, Xander felt caught in an infinite loop. He thought mainly of two things, his mother and David, and how he could help them both.

He practiced with his energy, trying to find ways to use it to help both of their clouds. He tried for what seemed like endless hours to improve his mother's cloud and even tried some new things, but always without success, at least in the way he wanted to succeed. He even tried forcing his energy into hers, hoping he could break apart, dissolve, or absorb the energy patterns he knew were associated with her sickness. Nothing he did seemed to have any effect on the cancer, although it sometimes seemed to aid his mother in other ways. He found he could help reduce or alleviate her headaches and nausea, but he always ended up feeling frustrated and disappointed. He would exhaust himself by manipulating his energy and then have to experience a letdown as he watched how short-lived any positive effects were on her.

Attempts at working with David's cloud were more successful, promising even, but external changes to David's wellness were slow to happen. Xander was pleased with the gradual expansion of the background color and the continual diminishing of the swamp, but he would have liked to see the same, obvious changes in David's sullen silences and dark moods. If not for the occasional grin or sarcastic jokes that Xander noticed David was making more frequently, Xander would have underestimated the importance of the association between David and his energy cloud. Still, he continued to let his own energy flow into the soft blue background to displace the brown sludge, all the while wondering why his attempts were not working on his mother.

David continued to make it to the meet-ups and to interact with Xander, though the interaction was minimal at first. They both would stand or sit by their mothers as the group went through the few minutes of ritual, and then they would head off together to walk the perimeter, only talking once in a while. Xander appreciated the silence as much as David, but for different reasons. It gave him time to focus on using his energy to intermingle with David's and expand the background color. When they did talk, they spoke about various things. Sometimes one would point out something in the park, and at other times one would ask the other what he thought about something. Xander didn't know whether what they shared counted as any kind of real relationship, but whatever it was, it worked for them.

When Xander's fourteenth birthday rolled around, it landed on a meet-up day. Tracy knew Xander would never demand a party, and she was always a bit disappointed because of it, so she took full advantage of the situation. She tried to play it off to Xander as casually as she could, but Xander could see and feel her restraining her excitement and did not do anything to squelch it. She compromised by not going all out and only brought a cake with one candle and some punch. Most of the other kids were excited by the cake, and most of the parents were perturbed at Tracy for not telling them in advance so they could bring a gift. Tracy shrugged off the blame, claiming that there was no precedence for birthdays during a meet-up, though it did little to placate the parents.

After lunch, the obligatory singing and candle blowing, and devouring of the cake, Xander thanked everyone and headed off with David. They were both quiet for a couple of laps, both quite full from the meal and cake. Xander walked with his head bowed and was enjoying the feel of the sun on his arms and neck. He was noticing that, for some weeks now, he and David had developed a matching stride when they walked that wasn't too long or quick for Xander's shorter legs. These days, he allowed his energy to flow into David's when they were together. David's cloud was looking lighter now and David himself seemed improved. Xander was hoping the improvement would continue when David broke the silence.

"I feel a little bit better."

He hadn't stopped walking or even turn toward Xander, but Xander looked at him and saw that David's face was relaxed and that he seemed to be breathing easily.

"Sorry I didn't get you anything. I didn't know it was your birthday."

"It's no big deal. I asked my mother not to tell anyone. I don't think birthdays are special, anyway."

"Yeah. They're as crappy as the rest."

Xander shook his head. "That's not what I meant."

He saw David turn his head toward him, waiting to hear what he did mean.

"I just meant… a birthday is just a day and every day is as good as a birthday. I meant it as a good thing."

David was still looking at him. "Hmm. Maybe."

They walked on until it was time to go and then helped their parents pack up. Xander closed the trunk and saw David standing by the passenger door. Xander walked over to him and stood in front of him, waiting to hear what he had to say.

David stood with his hands in his front pockets and looked around and toward his feet before his eyes met Xander's. He looked down again and said, "See you, Xander. Thanks."

He turned and walked away even before Xander's "bye" was heard.

Xander watched David and his cloud all the way to his van. He really was feeling better. Without realizing it, Xander thought, David had given him the best birthday gift he could have possibly given.

CHAPTER 24

For Xander, the next two years passed as an unbalanced mix of blurry months that whizzed by and elongated days that seemed to last for weeks. He kept busy with reading and other unschooling activities and meet-ups, learning to drive, and spending countless hours learning more about the energy that he saw surrounding every living thing. Though he learned a lot by reading about the world of quantum physics and mechanics, his belief that all energy was connected was born through his own experimenting. The toxic treatments had stifled the spread and growth of his mother's cancer but had not stopped it, and Xander was determined to find a way to heal her by helping her heal her energy cloud.

He had learned through his experiences working with David's cloud that he couldn't force a change in another's energy, but he could influence it to change. Trying smaller experiments on his mother, his aunt, and some of the unschooling group members, he found that the success of influencing another's energy cloud depended on how open the other person was to changing their own thinking. If the person was stubborn or too skeptical or just plain fearful of change, any impact by Xander's energy would be hindered or prevented. His aunt Rebecca, for instance, was an example of a person who was not very open to changing her thinking.

Xander tried on several occasions to use his energy to stop or lessen the intensity of an argument between his mother and his aunt. When he would allow his energy to flow to his mother's cloud, her cloud would usually meld with Xander's, and she would start to calm herself. Unfortunately, he had no such success when he tried to repeat the process with his aunt.

Xander saw his aunt Rebecca's cloud as being tightly knit. No matter how hard he concentrated or how much of his energy he allowed to flow into hers, her cloud would always reject his energy.

Another thing he learned about his energy was that he could use it to affect other energy at times when he couldn't even see the other cloud. He figured that out by speaking with David. He and David had become friends, or at least as close to friends as two relatively unsociable people can be. Once in a while, they would even talk by phone, although it was usually when Tracy was not up to driving and wanted Xander to ask for a ride. Even during the short telephone conversations, Xander was able to sense David's cloud by concentrating on it. Xander was sure he could do it even if they weren't on the phone, though he would not be able to validate any changes without hearing David talk. He found he could improve David's mood, at least a little, by picturing his own energy flowing into David's. Even if he couldn't see the cloud, he was able to feel it, and that was enough to permit the flow. Xander realized that the more he helped improve David's cloud, the larger the impact and the longer the changes lasted. Gradually, and thanks in large part to Xander's energy, David's whole demeanor had become more positive.

The energy work he did with David, and more so with his mother, was stressful and draining. Xander also cleaned, cooked, and did whatever else he could for his mother. She was often exhausted and would sleep or rest at all hours of the day, giving Xander plenty of time to himself. So he sought outlets to distract himself. It was much easier for him to do that once he was able to drive. The flexibility of unschooling allowed him to attend driving school during the day, when most kids were in school, so he finished quickly, passed his driving test, and got his license. Xander really enjoyed driving and the feeling of independence it gave him. He had his own books, but he still enjoyed driving to the public library and reading in a different environment from his house. Sometimes, he would bring his laptop and sit for hours at a coffee house, sipping tea while reading about various energy-related topics.

One morning, after what seemed like an exceptionally long night doing energy work with his mother while she fought pain and nausea, his need for a change in environment overpowered his need for sleep. He checked on his mother one last time to ensure she was asleep and resting as comfortably as possible, then grabbed the keys from the counter and left the house. He drove to his favorite coffee house. Rather than his laptop, he had brought a journal that he had been using to make notes about energy clouds and his work with them. He periodically reviewed his notes, hoping to find a connection or to learn something that would help him help his mother heal herself.

He picked up the green tea with honey he had ordered and had just sat down in a seat by the window when he had a familiar feeling in his own energy cloud. He looked around and traced the source of the feeling to someone sitting alone at a table near the opposite corner. He couldn't see who it was, since the person was wearing a ball cap and was looking down at a magazine, so the bill of the hat covered the face. Xander knew who it was without having to see her face, and even if he hadn't seen the long, blonde ponytail flowing out from the loop in the back of her cap. He could tell by the tickle in his energy cloud and by confirmation with his own eyes when he saw the true blue energy swirling about her.

Excited and nervous, he stood and walked over to the table. He stopped behind the chair opposite the person, grinning and waiting. The girl tilted her head up just enough for Xander to see her face.

"Aren't you going to sit down?" she said with a pleasant smile.

Without answering or taking his eyes off of hers, he sat down, putting his book and tea in front of him. The scene felt surreal to Xander, as he lost himself in the blue of her cloud and in her light brown eyes. He felt warmth and peace radiating from her cloud, and he wanted to sit there forever, basking in the feeling. He looked at her cloud and realized there were no separations between the swirls like there were in his mother's or David's clouds. It was a field of blue, slowly and gracefully moving in waves around her.

"What's your name?"

Xander's empirical senses reconnected, and his eyes refocused on hers. "Xander. What's yours?"

"I'm Serenity," she said, sipping her drink.

Serenity. What a perfect name, Xander thought. He looked again at the tranquil blue field that made up her energy cloud. His own was mostly blue, but various shades of blue, and it also contained hints of other colors at times. It moved slowly, too, but not as slowly or as gracefully as Serenity's.

"So, you can see them, too," she stated.

Xander broke his stare at her cloud. "Energy clouds. Yes, I can see them, too," he said.

He remembered her admitting to seeing his when they first met at the pool ten years before. *She probably doesn't even remember me from there, but maybe she does from the ice cream shop. That was only a couple of years--*

"I do remember you. We saw each other at the pool and at the ice cream shop."

Xander could feel his heart beating hard in his chest. He wondered if she had just read his thoughts.

"Energy clouds. Hmm," Serenity said, seeming to ponder the term. "I like it... but I still call them auras. Your aura's always blue. Like mine." She took another sip of her drink and resumed flipping through pages in her magazine.

Xander's grin, which was lost for a second in his amazement of Serenity, returned.

"I've called them energy clouds since I was a kid," he said.

"We're still kids," she said without looking up.

Xander was intrigued and puzzled by her. "I meant when I was younger. A little kid."

Serenity looked up at him and grinned. "Well, I have to get going."

Disappointment must have been clearly expressed on Xander's face, because Serenity laughed out loud when she looked up at him. Xander was shocked and fearful that she might walk out, and he would lose her for a third time. She was an enigma to him, and he didn't want her to go out of his life. For the first time in his life, he tasted desperation.

"Wait. Do you have to leave right now?" he pleaded.

He didn't notice she had taken a pen out of her backpack and was writing on a napkin.

"No, but I want to." She handed him the napkin with her phone number showing. "Give me a call when you're free and we can meet up again."

She smiled at Xander and looked at his cloud once more, then stood up and walked toward the door.

"I'm free now," Xander called after her.

She just chuckled and glanced at him, and then walked out.

Xander watched her walk outside along the glass side of the shop until she was out of sight. He was hoping she'd look in the window at him and see him watching her, but she didn't. He reached for her with his senses and could feel the warm, comfortable feeling of her cloud fading in the distance. He looked down at the table and wrapped his hands around his cup, its warmth a cheap substitution for the feeling he had just lost.

He looked at the napkin she had given him. She had simply written *Serenity* and her phone number. She didn't even include her last name. That didn't matter, Xander concluded. He had her number, so he would be able to see her again.

He would call her. Soon.

CHAPTER 25

Xander had never felt this excited before. He didn't want to wait to call Serenity, but he forced himself to hold off until the next day. Not sure whether she attended public school, he waited until the mid-afternoon to call her. Just waiting to call her was difficult enough, but he was truly disappointed when the many rings turned into a voicemail message.

The message was brief and simple. "You've reached my voicemail. Leave a message if you want."

She didn't include her name, but there was no mistaking her voice. The beep sounded before Xander could think of what to say.

"Hi. It's Xander. Um… we met yesterday," he said, feeling a little foolish and self-conscious. "Anyway, I was wondering if you wanted to meet up sometime this week." Xander thought of a plan but wasn't able to think of anything original.

"I thought we could grab a drink and walk through a park. Call me back when you can, please." He wasn't happy with his message, but it was done.

Just before he disconnected, he added, "You can text me, too."

He left his room to check on his mom and found her sitting at the kitchen table with some tea.

"Hey, you. Did I hear you talking to someone?" Tracy said with a smile.

"Just leaving a message for a friend," Xander answered.

His mother's smile transformed into a suspicious grin as she raised one eyebrow. "A friend?"

Xander snickered in an uncommon display of playfulness for him. "A new friend, and yes, she's a girl. We met at the coffee house yesterday."

He knew this information would tickle his mother. He was right. Tracy beamed. Not just because Xander had met a girl, but she could tell Xander must be feeling happy. Even she, his mother, rarely saw him wearing an expression that showed any emotion.

"What's your new friend's name?" Tracy asked, sipping her tea to keep herself from smiling. She had never known Xander to be self-conscious, but she didn't want to take the chance in case Xander thought her smile was teasing.

"Serenity," Xander answered.

He thought her name was as beautiful as she was and, suddenly, she became visible in his imagination as the memory of their recent meeting played in his mind. He remembered the straw color of her ponytail, her caramel eyes, and her smile. He was picturing her true blue cloud and trying to feel the familiar tickle in his senses when he remembered where he was and jolted back to the present.

He looked at his mother and saw her smiling and staring at him. He then did experience being self-conscious and decided to change the subject. He had come to realize that time seemed to slow when he dwelled in the past or thought about the future, but he wanted time to pass quickly right now. He wanted to feel his phone vibrate in his pocket and feel the excitement of talking to Serenity again. Xander needed to change the subject and think about something, anything else other than Serenity.

"How are you feeling?" he asked his mother.

Tracy recognized her son's deliberate attempt to change the subject, but also knew his question was sincere. "I'm doing okay. Just tired."

She was telling the truth at the moment, and looked directly into Xander's eyes when she spoke, hoping he would be convinced and not ask any more questions about her health.

It didn't matter though, as Xander could see by her cloud that the cancer was worsening. What had once been merely tan specks had grown and coalesced, and her energy was now saturated with a thick, slow-moving tan color. He also guessed that his mother did not want to talk about it. They sat together for a couple of minutes in silence, both not wanting to talk about what interested the other.

Wanting to keep himself distracted, Xander kept his focus on his mother. Ever since he had known she was sick, really sick, he had wanted to share what he had learned about energy clouds with her. Something had always stopped him in the past from sharing with her what he could do, but he thought the timing could be right now. At least, he hoped it would be.

"Mother… I want to tell you something," he said, looking at her with more determination than she had ever seen from him.

She removed her hands from around her mug of tea and placed them in her lap to give him her full attention, and Xander could tell she was trying to ignore any other thoughts she was having.

"For a long time now, actually for most of my life, I have been able to see…" He paused for a moment, unsure of how to word what he wanted to say. "… Auras. Energy… around people. And, well, around animals and plants, too."

He watched her and waited for a reaction. She wore no expression and was processing the new information, and it reminded him of himself. Xander decided to take advantage of the continuing silence and give her more details before she decided whether or not to believe him.

"That's not all." He paused to ensure he still had her attention. "Sometimes I can manipulate other's energy to make them… to help them feel differently. To feel better."

He watched her as she took in the information. She was blinking more than usual, and Xander thought he may have overloaded her. In any case, she was still not talking, so Xander continued.

"I've done it successfully before… but I've learned that I only have so much influence over another person's energy. The other person still has ultimate control over what their energy does."

He stopped for a couple of seconds and his eyes dropped to the table. "I haven't been able to help you."

He looked up and Tracy saw that his eyes were watery.

"I see colors in energy, and I can tell which colors are good and which are not. Sometimes I can help move the bad colors around so the good ones can take over."

Now a single drop of water spilled over each of his eyelids, and his voice sounded a little strained as he went on. "I've tried and tried to help you, but no matter what I do... you keep getting worse."

Tracy's own eyes filled with tears at her son's sadness, though other thoughts were racing through her mind. *That explains so much*, she thought. She had always made excuses to other adults for Xander not making eye contact. *No, he was not autistic, he was just shy and that's why he tends to look above or around people instead of looking them in the eyes.*

She felt momentary relief, but then she had a fearful thought to replace what she had previously believed.

Great. He's not autistic, but he sees things. She focused on Xander and saw him blink away his few tears as his usual, blank expression fell into place.

She wondered how he knew she was getting worse. She was doing everything she could to appear strong, at least in front of him. Plus, she was doing everything the doctor recommended and almost everything her know-it-all sister ordered her to do. She was eating healthy, keeping as active as she could despite the nasty side effects brought on by the toxic treatment she was receiving, and she was maintaining a positive attitude.

Could he actually be doing what he said he was doing? *He had always had a remarkable insight into people*, she thought. *Perhaps this was how.* She knew he was waiting patiently to know what she thought of his confession. Whether or not she believed that he could see and manipulate energy. Tracy herself didn't know if she believed. *It's like a superpower... what kid didn't wish for a super power? Xander just had a stronger imagination than most. Of course, that still didn't account for his insight about people and his understanding of issues way beyond his maturity.* Her internal monologue continued until she realized she still had not responded out loud.

"Honey, the doctor would have told me if... if I was getting worse."

His expression remained unchanged, and she realized she still hadn't addressed his... power.

"Look, I believe you if you say you can... see energy, but you can't be expected to be able to cure cancer," she said.

"I know that. That's why I'm telling you."

Xander had readied himself for her response. He suspected she didn't believe him, but he felt he had no other choice than to try to make her believe.

"I can help, but I can't do it. You have to cure yourself."

Xander continued despite Tracy's obvious skepticism. "I can teach you how. It's really not that hard... you'll just need to practice a lot."

Once again, and to Tracy's surprise, his face took on an expression. This time he was the one pleading. "You just have to believe!"

Tracy left her chair and dropped to her knees next to Xander and hugged him close. Xander hugged her back and shed a couple more tears. He could tell his mother was crying, too. She pulled away, but moved her hands to his shoulders and looked into his eyes with her head touching his.

"I'll try," she said, sniffing. "I'll really try."

Then they hugged each other again, each understanding that they didn't know how many more hugs there would be.

CHAPTER 26

THIS had been a strange week for Xander. He had always experienced a wide range of emotions but had dealt with and reacted to them differently than most people… up until this week. This week, he had shed more tears and felt more rampant emotions than he had in the past decade. For starters, he had experienced impatience, which turned to irritation and then to anger because Serenity had not yet called him back. He had left a message every single day since they had seen each other. His anger was further fueled by the humiliation he felt at having left six messages. He knew he would appear desperate and, worse than that, it would be the truth. He was desperate to talk to her and to see her again. He argued with himself about why she would give him her number and then ignore his calls.

Then there was his mother and her cancer. It had not gotten any better, and he was not surprised. He felt she was humoring him when she said she was trying to change her energy. He could clearly see that she was not really trying. There was absolutely no change in the color or substance of her cloud at all, no different movement even when he was watching her at times she claimed she was trying to see or move it. Her lack of faith in what would help her was frustrating to him… and scary.

He had just finished a tedious half hour with his mother, trying to teach her how to sense her own energy. She told him she had been feeling better since they had been working together, but Xander wasn't convinced. It was possible that she did, but that was nothing more than the placebo effect and was more for his benefit than for hers. He knew it wouldn't last unless she came to believe she was healing herself. Xander understood the futility of that session and said that was enough for the day.

He had intended to read, but was unable to focus on the words on the screen. He then attempted to meditate on the couch, but his frustration from his mom's ruse and the bitterness from not being able to read made meditation impossible. He let out a deep sigh and thought for a moment about what he could do that didn't require the use of his brain. A solution presented itself in the form of the nearby remote control. He grabbed it from the coffee table and turned on the television to a channel that only aired documentaries.

A documentary about the Marianas Trench was being broadcast, which was perfect for Xander. He had already learned just about everything that had been published on the topic, and so he didn't have to try to absorb any new information. He could let his mind rest and was able to just be.

He felt an itch on his thigh and realized his phone had vibrated. Excited with anticipation, he pulled it from his front pocket and saw the text message alert on the screen just before it faded. He unlocked his screen to read the text. As he had hoped, it was from Serenity.

"Wanna meet?" was all it read.

Xander was simultaneously surprised, elated, and dissatisfied. He had hoped for, no, expected an apology. Either that or an elaborate excuse about why she had taken so long to return his message. Now that he thought about it, he realized she wasn't necessarily responding to his messages even now. He felt irritated again, but the joy in hearing from her overpowered his angst. He typed his reply.

"Yes! Drink and a walk?"

"Sure. 30 minutes okay?"

Xander assumed she meant that she was asking if they should meet at the same coffee house in thirty minutes.

"Yes. See you then."

He turned off the television and threw the remote on the couch, then went to find his mother. The coffee shop was ten minutes away, so he had time to dress and brush his teeth. His mom was lying down in her bed and reading a paperback.

"Do you mind if I go for a walk with a friend?" he asked, leaning on her doorframe.

She laid her book down on her chest and smirked at him. "With Serenity?"

"Yes, with Serenity," Xander answered.

"Go on. Have a good time," she said and shooed him away with her hand.

"Thanks, Mother."

"Tell her hi for me," she yelled, as he had already turned and headed to get dressed.

CHAPTER

XANDER was prompt, but Serenity was not. He became anxious after waiting for twenty minutes without seeing or hearing from her. He was just about to text her when he felt an internal nudge, then looked up and saw her walk into the shop.

He would always remember seeing her at that moment. She was not wearing a ball cap this time, but had her hair down, falling in gorgeous waves over her shoulders and onto an unflattering, gray sweatshirt with the name *Seattle* printed on it. The sweatshirt hung halfway over her faded denim cut-off shorts. She wore red-and-white flip-flops on her feet, below legs which Xander assumed were so toned from athletics. Giving Xander a small wave, she walked straight to the counter to order a drink. Again, Xander felt a sting of disappointment. He had wanted to buy her drink. *Get over it*, he told himself, and he waved back with a grin.

Xander heard Serenity order a small soy mocha with extra chocolate. He watched her, but she didn't look toward him once until after she had received her drink and turned to join him. She took a big sip of her coffee as she walked over to the table where Xander was sitting. He always had to wait for a drink to cool off before attempting anything but the smallest sip, but he noticed that the temperature didn't seem to affect her in the slightest. She sat down across from him with a big smile.

"Hi, there!" she said.

Xander couldn't help himself from smiling. Her positivity was contagious.

"Hi!" he answered, trying to sound equally as cheerful. "I was thinking we could take our drinks to the park across the street." He pointed to the park.

"Okay," she shrugged, stood up, and started walking for the door. Xander hurried after her since she gave no sign of waiting for him.

They walked across the street and into the park without talking. Xander took small sips from his tea while trying to think of what to say. He was not in his element. In fact, he felt like he was in a foreign land and experiencing a culture altogether new to him. Serenity, on the other hand, looked to Xander to feel quite comfortable. She walked and looked around as if they were taking in a stroll around her own back yard. He didn't know why, but Xander felt like he was losing a battle. He wondered what he could say that would interest her, but also felt like time was of the essence and that he would lose what little attention she was paying him if he didn't speak up soon.

Soaking in that fear, he decided that saying anything at this point would be better than remaining silent. "So… do you go to school?" Even he thought the question sounded dull.

Serenity scoffed. "Yeah… I go to school. Don't you?"

Xander rolled his eyes, feeling inept. "Not really. I unschool."

"Unschool," she repeated. "So, you do the opposite of go to school."

"I guess so."

"That's cool," she said, not needing further explanation.

Xander was glad for that, not because he was ashamed of being unschooled; it was just that he would rather talk about her. First, though, he needed to ask her something.

"Why didn't you get back to me after I called?" Xander asked, trying to sound curious and indifferent.

"I did. I sent you a text, remember?"

"Yeah… almost a week later and after I left six messages."

He immediately regretted bringing attention to the additional, desperate voicemails he had left her.

"Yeah… what was that about?" Serenity asked.

Xander thought fast and tried to play it off as a joke. "I just wanted to make sure you got my message," he said with a grin.

"I got it and I texted you," she said, shrugging. "I didn't say when I would get back to you."

"I just assumed I would hear from you sooner."

"You assumed," she repeated. "Assumptions, expectations… it doesn't make sense to have them when you have no control over the outcome."

Xander was miffed, but he knew she was right.

They both were drawn to the sound of a giggle up ahead and identified the source as a couple of joggers approaching them. Two very fit-looking young adults were laughing at something funny and matching pace. The man had his shirt off, and sweat gleamed off his muscles. The young woman looked equally as in shape and attractive. They seemed to be a couple, since the man lightly touched the woman's waist, moving her in front of him so they could pass around Xander on the grass.

Serenity looked over her shoulder to watch the couple return to a side-by-side formation and hold hands for a few steps.

"They're hot!" Serenity exclaimed, turning back to face forward.

Xander snickered and his brow furrowed. He felt a sudden irritation at her remark and then wondered why. *At the man for… what? For being healthy and attractive, or because he attracted Serenity's attention?*

"Why would you say that?"

"Why not?" she answered.

She looked at Xander and saw his face wrinkled up in obvious disapproval.

"Oh, what? You didn't think they both had beautiful bodies?" she asked.

"I hadn't really noticed," Xander replied.

It was a lie, and it was strange to him. He suddenly felt like he was in an alien environment. Or possessed. *I don't lie*, he said to himself, but he knew he had just lied. The answer came to him almost immediately, but he was hesitant to admit it.

I'm jealous. We're just walking together, and I'm jealous of a passing stranger.

He was experiencing a storm of unusual emotions that rendered him temporarily speechless. As if she could sense his internal struggle, Serenity added, "What can I say… I appreciate beauty no matter what form it takes."

Xander thought some more. *Well, she did compliment them both… and she didn't say anything crude. Plus, she has no reason to lie to me. Even though I lied to her.*

He did his best to rationalize ways to make himself feel better. He felt for her energy cloud. It was as blue as always. No hint of anything else. Serenity pushed Xander's shoulder, making him veer off the path.

"Oh, get over it. You're wasting the moment."

The shove only served to irritate Xander further, but as her words settled in his mind, their meaning became clear and he calmed himself.

She's right, he thought. *I am wasting the moment.*

He took some deep breaths and, one by one, focused on his empirical senses. After, he placed his concentration on his energy and consciously moved it to come in contact with Serenity's energy cloud. It seemed to exude warmth, health, strength, and peace. He could feel his own energy swirling in an inward motion, as if it was absorbing hers.

"I've been able to see auras for as long as I can remember," she said, breaking the silence and, once again, seeming to read Xander's thoughts.

So, she's like me, but she doesn't seem quite as different. She seems more… normal.

"Did you ever tell anyone else?" he asked.

"No. Did you?"

"Just my mother. She pretends to believe, but she really doesn't." Xander felt a twinge of sadness as his thoughts went to his mother and the cancer.

Serenity stopped, turned to him and asked, "Are you okay?"

She was looking at Xander with an expression of empathy, as if she could feel his sadness. Her reaction did more to distract Xander than anything.

"Are you reading my mind?" he asked.

"No, silly, but I can feel your energy cloud shift when your feelings do."

She began walking again and Xander caught up and matched pace. He smiled at her having said "energy cloud" instead of "aura." They walked for a while and made small talk. They discussed common interests and books they both had read, and Xander did not want their time to end, but it did. They had made several laps around the park and were nearing the coffee shop when Serenity turned and started toward the street.

"I'm gonna go."

Xander thought quickly of a way to set another date to see her again. "Would you like to do this again sometime? We can go to another park if you like, or we can do something else."

He knew he sounded a little desperate, but he didn't care.

"Okay."

Xander was disappointed at her apparent lack of enthusiasm. *More of my expectations*, he thought.

"When and what would you like to do?" he asked.

"Not sure. But this was fun. Thanks!" she said and started walking away.

"Well… should I call or text you?" Xander called after her.

"Sure."

"When?"

"I don't care."

Her words crushed Xander. He stood there on the sidewalk, watching her walk away. He didn't know where she was going, where she lived, or even her last name. So many new feelings enveloped and overwhelmed him, he was not sure what to do. He felt like he had to drag himself to the car, and then he drove home and flopped face down onto his bed. He replayed the last minutes with Serenity over in his mind, trying to rationalize something positive in her departing words. He was so drained and emotionally stressed, he fell asleep within a few minutes, watching his imagination show Serenity walk away from him once again.

CHAPTER

XANDER spent the next two days trying to make sense of his afternoon with Serenity. He had thought they had hit it off and were getting along nicely. He tried to remember when that comfortable feeling had changed; then he remembered. It was when she made the remark about the couple they saw jogging. She had complimented their physiques, and then he had become irritated… no, jealous. He had been jealous for the first time in his life and over someone he barely knew. Afterward, she had told him to get over it and that he was wasting the moment. He knew she had been right, but what puzzled him was that he already understood that before it had happened, but he let it happen anyway.

I have to remember… I can't think rationally while I'm feeling that strongly.

He also thought about her uncanny ability to know what he was thinking. Serenity had said she couldn't read minds but could feel his energy cloud shift when his feelings did. He had tried to see and feel shifts in other people's energy, but he must only be able to detect very obvious changes, whereas she was able to pick up on subtle ones. He made a mental note to ask her to teach him how to do that the next time they were together. That was, if they would be together in the future. Xander was having a difficult time coming to grips with the way she had left him. She seemed indifferent toward whether or not he should call her and when, despite the fact that she seemed to enjoy his company as well as he enjoyed hers.

Well, perhaps not quite as well as I did, Xander thought.

"I don't care," she had said. Her words still stung Xander. She seemed okay with him contacting her and with them doing something together again, she just didn't seem very enthusiastic about it… or even very interested.

Like she doesn't care, Xander thought, feeling dejected again.

His consciousness drifted back and forth between emotions and rational thinking for a time. He would feel low and sorry for himself as his imagination created scenarios about the situation, and then his brain would overpower his feelings and he would remind himself that he was, once again, making assumptions and having expectations. He knew there could be countless reasons why she said what she had said, and many of them — most of them — might have nothing whatsoever to do with him. Once he caught the different parts of himself playing internal tennis, he focused on his breathing and then did his best to meditate by cycling his attention through his physical senses.

After doing that for about fifteen minutes, he felt better and let his brain engage again. "Should I call her?" and "When should I call her?" were the two questions on his mind, although the second question was a clear sign that he had already made up his mind about the first. He had just seen her the day before yesterday, *so would today be too soon to call her?* he wondered. When he considered her closing remarks to him, he doubted she was giving it much thought at all, if any. So, he decided there was no reason to wait if he wanted to call her, so he did.

Her voicemail answered after several rings, and Xander found himself annoyed and impatient. Luckily, he caught himself and was able to leave a message that wasn't laden with sarcasm or irritation. He forced himself to wait a few seconds before talking in order to relax himself and release any expectations he may have had with regard to her response when she listened to his message.

"Hi. This is Xander. I was hoping we could—"

His message was cut off by a beep. He glanced at his phone and saw it was Serenity calling and he answered.

"Hi, there," he said, smiling.

He was excited and had momentarily forgotten every negative thing in his life.

"Hi. I'm in the bath and didn't dry my hands quickly enough to answer after I saw it was you."

Xander felt elated. She screened her calls, but answered while in the bath when she saw it was him! Beaming, he stood up and paced around his bed as he talked.

"Hey. Do you want to call me back after your bath?" he asked, wanting her to say no.

"If I didn't want to talk I wouldn't have answered it. What's up?"

Xander could hear small splashes in the background that helped his imagination distract him. "Oh, um, I was just calling to see if you wanted to go to the park tomorrow."

"Not really," she answered, stopping Xander dead in his tracks. "How about we go on a hike instead?" she asked.

Xander resumed his pacing and his excitement. "That'd be terrific!" he said.

Serenity sensed his giddiness and let out a small giggle.

"Should we meet somewhere, or..." Xander began.

"Can you pick me up? We could head up to the foothills about ten and each pack a lunch."

At that moment, she could have asked Xander for anything and he would have agreed to it, despite his poor attempt to seem aloof.

"Sounds like a plan."

She gave him her address, which he placed under the car keys in a bowl on the kitchen counter. Not that it mattered, as he had already memorized it.

So, this is what it must feel like to be intoxicated. It was all Xander could think to describe his current emotion.

Smiling, he invited his mother to watch a movie with him and volunteered to make the popcorn. Tracy chose a romantic comedy for them to watch and Xander pretended to protest, though it was obvious even to his mother that the genre suited him just fine.

CHAPTER 29

NEITHER Xander nor Tracy could keep from smiling the next morning, despite Tracy's obvious pain and discomfort from nausea. Xander, of course, had told Tracy his plans for the day, and she seemed as happy as he was. They ate breakfast together, but Xander was distracted with anticipation and excitement at the thought of seeing Serenity again.

For Tracy, it was the joy of seeing her son behaving as though he was happy instead of her having to ask and taking his word for it. Xander made breakfast and offered to do dishes, but Tracy insisted he not be late picking up Serenity and said she would do them. He left only after she promised to leave them for him to do later if she felt too tired.

Xander arrived at Serenity's house a few minutes before ten, so he waited in his car across the street. At precisely ten o'clock, he knocked on her front door. A tall, slender man with light brown hair that was graying at the temples opened the door.

"Xander? Hey, I'm Marcus, Serenity's dad. Come on in," he said, opening the door wide and gesturing for Xander to enter.

Xander noticed and appreciated the casualness with which Marcus introduced himself and felt only the tiniest bit disappointed that he still didn't know Serenity's last name.

"Hi," Xander answered and extended his hand to shake while stepping into the entryway.

Marcus smiled with amusement as he shook Xander's hand and closed the door.

"Serenity said to tell you she'd be down in a minute. You can grab a seat until she's ready," he said as they walked past the entryway into the small living room. He excused himself with a wave and left the room.

"Thanks," replied Xander with a nod as he sat down and looked around at the eclectic décor surrounding him. There was no obvious theme, save for several knick-knacks and small items that looked to be from Europe and Asia. It appeared that someone in the family had done some traveling, and Xander wondered if Serenity had been one of the tourists.

He felt a familiar and welcomed tickle as he heard someone coming down the stairs. Serenity came into sight, and they both smiled when they saw each other.

"Hey. Ready?" she asked, clapping her hands together.

Xander was captivated as his eyes took in the Serenity's physical attributes and his internal sense met with her energy. She was dressed in boots, cargo shorts, and a tank top, displaying her slender, athletic figure. Her hair was back up in a ponytail again and hanging out the back of her baseball cap, and her energy cloud made it look like she was standing against a blue backdrop. The sheer representation of power that was her true blue energy never ceased to amaze Xander. He thought she was beautiful, but he was attracted as much or more to her energy than to her looks.

"Yeah," Xander replied, standing up and following her to the door.

The drive from Serenity's house to the base of the foothills trail where they would start their hike took about forty-five minutes, and Xander was glad for the extra time to talk with Serenity. He did not want to waste time with small talk, but had been anxiously waiting to ask her more about her own experiences with using her energy. Specifically, he wanted to ask her to teach him how to interpret the subtle changes which he had not yet been able to detect. They had just merged onto the freeway when Xander jumped right in with his first question.

"When we were at the park, I asked if you could read my mind and you said no, but that you could feel my energy shift with my feelings... how did you learn to do that?"

Xander was anticipating her answer and was excited just to be talking to her, and he had to mentally balance himself in order to pay attention to the fact that he was driving. Serenity was looking straight ahead and seemed to be contemplating her answer.

"Hmmm… I've never thought about putting words to it," she began. "It's not something I deliberately tried to learn. One day I just realized that I could do it."

She turned to look at Xander. "How are you able to move your energy with mine?"

For the first time in his life, Xander blushed. He was mortified that she knew their energies had come in contact with each other. Serenity laughed at him, which made him blush even more.

"Don't worry. I don't feel violated. I can see our… energy clouds… too, remember? I saw you make your energy swirl and draw my energy into your cloud," she said, sounding somewhat impressed. "I thought it was pretty cool."

That put Xander at ease a bit. "I can move mine around a little and sometimes move other people's energy."

"You can change other people's energy?" Serenity asked with a tone that Xander thought could have been genuine interest or judgment. He hoped it was the former and gave her the benefit of the doubt.

"No. Not change it. Just move it around," he said, calmly. "I used it to help move… unhealthy energy… out of the way so the other person's positive energy has a chance at expanding."

"Sounds kind of like what white blood cells do."

Xander thought about that and agreed it was a good analogy.

"Did it always work?" Serenity asked, and then added with a raised eyebrow, "Do you still do it?"

He remembered being able to widen the gaps in David's cloud to allow his background color to come through, but his failed attempts at doing anything to improve his mother's energy also sprang to his mind.

"No, I don't do it anymore."

"That's probably for the best," Serenity answered, but Xander was too deep in thought to hear it or think it strange.

"Besides, it didn't always work." Xander thought about his mother and felt frustrated and disappointed in himself. Also, he realized the conversation had gotten off track.

Detecting Xander's emotional dilemma, Serenity said, "Right there. I felt your energy shift. It felt like you were feeling sad or something. Feel your cloud and see if you can detect the difference."

Xander thought, *She did it again.* He tried to set aside his awe of Serenity's recent demonstration of her ability and sense his own energy. At first, all he could feel was the predominant blue, the normal feel for his cloud, though not a true blue like hers. He allowed his internal sense to move through and around the cloud, trying to notice anything. Realizing that any changes may have disappeared since he no longer was feeling the same emotions he was a minute ago, he was about to give up when two things happened. The first was that he detected the slightest variation in his energy cloud. Xander likened it to a hairline fracture, running from the center of himself to the perimeter of his cloud. It was barely noticeable and was fading fast, disappearing from the center out.

The second thing that happened was that he came close to colliding with the car in front of them.

"Xander!" Serenity shouted as she tried to make her seat recline from sheer force.

Xander's awareness shifted so he was focusing with his eyes again and saw that the line of cars in front had slowed and the brake lights were illuminated and seemed to be rapidly approaching him. He hit the brakes in time and was able to maintain a single car length of space from the car they were following. Serenity laughed and, after a few seconds, Xander joined her.

"Were you able to see it?" she said, chuckling.

"Yes, barely, but I saw something."

"Good. Just keep practicing," she said, and then added, "but I recommend you do it when you're not operating heavy equipment."

Xander faked a scowl and they both laughed again.

With traffic, the drive took an hour. Xander was feeling too happy to ask any more serious questions, so he and Serenity just enjoyed the ride, sometimes sharing personal stories that came to mind and sometimes just sitting in silence for minutes at a time. Xander wore a grin on his face the whole time.

Once they arrived at the trail head, they both ate half of a sandwich and they split an orange that Serenity had brought. They decided they would need some energy before the hike and would most likely be starving afterward, so they stowed the rest of their lunches, grabbed their waters, and started off.

It was a cloudy and muggy day, but there was a cool breeze that felt good against the sweat on Xander's face and arms. It was a six-mile round trip and rated as moderate, but Xander wasn't worried. In fact, he wasn't thinking too much about anything but Serenity. As they walked, they continued sharing memories and pointed out interesting things they spotted along the trail. Serenity was particularly fond of looking at mushrooms, so Xander kept a sharp eye out for different species, and ones that were unusually large or near perfect in appearance.

They also talked about energy. Xander shared all the experiences that stood out for him. He told her about when he first saw the glow from the spider and about his epiphany while at the science museum. He described in detail how he had tried to help David adjust his energy by widening the gaps in David's swamp-like cloud to allow the healthier background colors to shine through. Unsure why, he hesitated to share when his thoughts drifted to his mother and her cancer. The more he thought about it, the more he was sure he felt like a failure and he was embarrassed to admit it to Serenity.

Serenity told Xander about some of her experiences with energy as well. She had always been able to see them and learned to read them as she learned everything else.

"Understanding auras… energy clouds…" she corrected herself, "helped me understand people."

Xander was intrigued. He understood she could detect changes, and quickly—so quickly that he thought she had been reading his mind—but understanding people by those changes was something else.

"How do you mean?" he asked.

"It's kind of like a math formula. An equation, of sorts. I just factor in a sudden change in energy with the situation at hand, tone of voice, body language, and the words people choose. It's usually easy to tell when someone is mad or scared or sad, but when I started to see patterns in the combinations of the factors, I learned to piece together *why* people felt the way they did."

Xander listened intently, trying to absorb every word. He concentrated so hard on what she was saying, he sometimes lost his footing and came close to rolling his ankle on several occasions. He tried not to grunt or gasp when he did for fear she would stop talking, and so she continued.

"Not that it's an exact science, but for the most part I am able to get people." She stopped and looked up, tilting her head in thought. "I think understanding people helps me not judge them." She shrugged and resumed walking.

Xander caught himself before he plowed into her after her sudden stop and then had to quick-step to catch up with her.

"Plus, we're all really energy and no energy is bad."

Now Xander stopped. Serenity heard him stop and turned to face him.

"Some energy is bad," he said.

He felt a tinge of disgust as he thought about the mucky energy that had surrounded David and his mother's cancer represented by the thick, tan soup in her cloud. Knowing she did not understand what he was talking about, he reminded her about David's energy and, with a deep sigh, told her about his mother and the cancer.

Xander felt more bitter than sad at that moment, but his face remained expressionless. They stood where they were as he described what he saw as bad energy in his friend and his mother, and when he was finished, waited for the inevitable validation he expected to receive from Serenity. But none came.

"That's not bad energy, Xander. It's just energy. Energy is just the universe, and part of it forms things. Tangible things like stars, planets, plants, animals, and us, and intangible things like gasses, electricity, and auras. It's just in the case of auras, the energy can be... changed by thoughts and feelings."

Xander imagined her watching him and keeping her senses tuned to his cloud as she continued with her description.

"Water!" she said. "If you add coffee, milk, and chocolate, you have a mocha, but add dirt and you have mud. It's like that with auras or energy clouds or whatever you call the energy that makes up a living being. Thoughts and emotions can be something delicious... or they can be crap. Whether the energy surrounding a person is beautiful or crappy, their body just reacts accordingly."

Xander shook his head. "I've seen healthy-looking people with… dirty energy."

"That just means they may be physically healthy… for the moment, but their thoughts are not. And it won't be that way for too long. If their thoughts and emotions keep their energy dirty, their physical body will eventually match it."

Xander thought about what this meant with regard to his mother. He thought that she had stress that was common to adults, but nothing significant weighing her down. At least not as far as he knew.

Was it something from her past, he asked himself. *His father, their relationship—or was it something from even farther back? Something from her childhood?* She had never told him about any traumatic events, but she could have a secret.

Serenity walked forward until there was only about a foot of space between them. Xander's heart pounded as she neared and then felt to him as though it were trying to break free when she took both of his hands in hers.

"You can't control someone else's energy. You said so yourself." She looked down between them and then lifted her head until their eyes met once again.

"Do you know what causes the most problems with people? What people do to dirty and stain their own auras more than anything?"

Xander felt paralyzed in his body, and he braced himself for what he believed was going to be one of the most profound and important lessons he would ever learn.

"People don't love themselves" was all she said.

Serenity let go of Xander's hands, turned, and began walking. Xander hadn't wanted to lose the physical contact yet, but he savored the lingering feeling of elation as he forced his body into motion and followed behind her. A light rain cut through the mugginess and fell on them, rinsing their sweat and cooling their skin. As soon as they exited the trail, it was wide enough for them to walk side by side, and once Xander was next to her, she reached for his hand, which he was glad to give. They walked the short way to the car, both of them smiling and giving the other sideways glances.

Xander pulled the car up in front of Serenity's house and shut off the engine. Serenity unfastened her seat belt and turned sideways in her seat to face him.

"Look, you can't fix your mom's energy. You know that. And you choosing to feel sad or helpless or frustrated or angry won't help her or you."

"We don't choose how we feel," Xander said in defense, though he knew better.

"You're right. Not at first, but as soon as our brain engages and we can recognize what we are feeling, then it becomes a choice, and we can choose to feel something different."

Xander thought, *She's right again*, but didn't respond aloud.

"So, choose to be happy! That's what I do." Serenity leaned over and gave him a hard kiss on the cheek.

"Thank you for driving," she said, climbing out of the car and shutting the door behind her before Xander could respond. He watched her jog up her walk and disappear into her house. It had started raining harder, and his windows were fogging up, so he started the car and switched the air to defrost and the fan speed to high. So many thoughts raced through his head, foremost of which were the facts that she held his hand and kissed him. On the cheek, but still a kiss.

He pulled away from the curb and headed home. He was tired from the hike and drained from thinking and feeling. Her words echoed in his head all the way to his house, and he believed all of them. Words and meanings he would remember forever, but now he wanted to think about his mother. Serenity was right. He couldn't fix her, but maybe there was still a way to help her fix herself. He would find a way to make her believe in the energy, at least. If she believed, then he would somehow prove to her how energy influences her health. Lastly, he would tell her how to clean up her own energy, which would, in turn, restore her physical health. The bottom line was... he would have to teach her to love herself.

CHAPTER 30

Now Xander had two goals on which he spent his time. Working with his mother so she could learn to love and heal herself, and spending time with Serenity. Both endeavors proved difficult for him.

He knew he was going to have to ease into the process of helping his mother help herself, and a process it was. They would need to do several things in a specific order, the first of which was to get her to believe in the energy. That part seemed easy to do, since there was science backing up that the cells of living things are filled with energy. Of course, there were also documented studies on the existence of auras, complete with pictures to help prove to her that it wasn't just a belief for some people. Unfortunately, even when presented with scientific facts and empirical data, some people, including his mother, had a hard time understanding the true significance of the concept of energy surrounding a living being. She was an intelligent woman, but even her nods and feeble expressions of astonishment did not convince Xander that she truly understood.

One afternoon, after Xander provided his mother with detailed descriptions of what he had learned, seen, and done with energy, he thought he had finally found a way to get through to her. She was smiling and listening, although mostly out of courtesy, Xander guessed. He saw her rub her forehead with her fingers. He focused on her cloud and was able to see tiny variations that confirmed she had the onset of a headache.

"You're starting to get a headache."

She smiled. "It's nothing."

It's not nothing, thought Xander. *It's my chance to prove to you once and for all how your energy can be manipulated to help you.*

He was excited and concentrated all of his attention on their clouds. He had had enough practice for this to be a simple maneuver. He could see and feel tiny golden spots that were slowly spreading along the edge of her cloud, and he charged his cloud while moving it over those new spots in hers. Within a minute or two, he could see that most of the spots were gone and the remaining ones were fading. He reached across the kitchen table and took one of his mother's hands with both of his.

"Feel any better?" he asked, grinning.

"Actually, I do," she said, smiling back at him. "I always feel better when you're around."

Xander's grin stayed, but the hope which had produced it died. *This is going to be even harder than I thought.*

He wasn't having any better luck on the Serenity front. Most of his attempts to contact her resulted in a voicemail and a returned call a day or so later, if at all. He even tried just texting, but that only served to create more frustration when his messages weren't returned or, even worse, were returned with a one-word message into which he imagined an indifferent or negative tone. Xander wasn't sure what to think of their relationship, and the couple of times he had seen her in the several weeks after the hike did nothing to clarify it.

After many attempts to contact her and arrange another time to meet, Xander was finally successful, and they ended up going bowling. Xander thought that a mistake in hindsight, since he would have rather been alone with her or at least somewhere it was quiet enough to talk.

They also went on two more hikes. Xander was hoping for a repeat of their first hike, including and especially the hand-holding and the kiss. Of course, he had plans to elevate the status of her friendly kiss on the cheek to something more. Once again, however, reality did not match up with Xander's expectations, and he was disappointed. Serenity didn't act distant, but she made no attempts to be any closer than friends. Xander thought that surely after she had held his hands and kissed him, albeit a friendly kiss, she would be at least open to a deeper relationship with him. To Xander, Serenity seemed to have two sides. One side of her could seem so sweet and caring toward him, and the other side could seem indifferent, leaving him unsure whether she liked him at all. It seemed to all depend on the moment.

His confusion and frustration over the matter climaxed at the end of their second hike. Xander had been walking close enough to her to brush her hand with his as they swung their arms, hoping all the while that she would grab and hold his hand as it passed. She didn't grab or hold his hand, and she didn't pull away from it when they touched. She simply ignored it.

At last, Xander was fed up. He stopped on the trail and waited until she stopped and turned to face him.

"What is it with you?" he said.

Serenity didn't respond but simply stood and smiled at him, which Xander took as her being condescending.

"First you hold my hand. Then you kiss me. Then you don't answer my calls or texts for days. You said yes when I asked you to go bowling and hiking with me, so I assume you want to spend time with me, too, but then when we're together, you act as if we're just friends. I don't get it."

Xander had never felt like this before, like he had too much emotion and it was spiraling out of control in all directions.

"You seem upset," she said, walking toward him and still smiling.

"I guess I am." Without her coming back at him with a defense or argument of any kind, Xander felt foolish and tried to calm himself down.

"What have I told you about assumptions and expectations?" she asked. She moved closer to him and grabbed his hands like she did on their first hike.

"Can you read my mind?" she asked him.

Xander thought she was patronizing him and he felt more foolish than before. "Of course not," he said, averting his eyes down and away from hers.

She maneuvered her head and eyes until he finally looked at her.

"No. You can't read my mind. And since you haven't asked me anything, any conclusions you have drawn must be assumptions." She dropped his hands. "So in the future, I recommend you ask instead of—"

Xander cut her off to finish her sentence: "—assuming or having expectations."

"No," she corrected him. "Just don't assume. There is nothing wrong with having expectations, just as long as you remember that you can't control anything external to you and choose not to be disappointed if your expectations aren't met."

Xander wanted to think about what she said in more depth, but he understood the gist and wanted to seize the moment.

"Do you like me? You know, as more than a friend." He could tell by her smile that Serenity enjoyed hearing him say that and that she did like him.

"Yes, Xander. I like you, and as more than a friend."

Xander felt happier than he ever remembered feeling, if only for a second.

"But..." she continued, and Xander's heart, hope, and smile all dropped at the same time. "... you're not ready for a relationship. You haven't learned to fully love yourself yet."

Xander's ego, usually subdued, leaped out in front.

"How can you say that?" he said almost at a yell. "Now who's making assumptions?"

Serenity backed up a step. "It's not an assumption; it's an observation."

"An observation? How can you know that I don't fully love myself?"

He was doing everything he could to lower and calm his voice, but he felt a tremendous amount of pressure coming from within himself.

Serenity watched him restrain himself and waited to speak until she saw he had more control. "For starters, people who truly love themselves don't get jealous."

Xander remembered how he felt when she had complimented the attractive and fit couple they saw jogging.

"That's because people who truly love themselves don't care what other people think about them and don't need... aren't desperate for... a relationship with anyone other than themselves."

Xander didn't know what to say. He just stared at her... and loved her. She was amazing, and everything he wanted to be, so he made a commitment to himself that afternoon. He vowed to learn to fully love himself, but for the purpose of achieving the level of happiness and security that Serenity enjoyed, not to win her over.

Serenity giggled, turned, and started walking, calling over her shoulder, "Come on you big dork."

Xander followed obediently, thinking to himself that it would be that much better if he managed to win her over, too.

CHAPTER

XANDER continued to think about Serenity's words about self-love and about his promise to himself to make changes in his life to fulfill that promise. He set time aside every day to meditate on loving himself, usually for a few minutes when he first woke up, and then again just before he went to sleep. During his meditations, he would search for a strong feeling of love, usually through thinking about his mother, though sometimes he thought about Serenity. Focusing on the feeling, he would picture it as a bright blue light at the core of his being, expanding outward until there was nothing else. When this happened, he allowed himself to feel detached from the physical world. He would think of his body as a worldly object, his favorite object, and one he wanted to love and protect more than anything else. Then he would imagine his mind as a swirl in his energy cloud, and he would feel love for that, as well. In those moments of meditation, somehow he knew without any doubt that he was the same energy as everything, everywhere, at any time. He knew this not because he had read about quantum physics, but because he could feel it.

For weeks, he would think of his meditation time as sessions, and he would place value on them based on how much time he spent during each session. A session could take an hour to an hour and a half, however much time it took for Xander to imagine the bright blue light filling up his body, inch by inch through every extremity, and only after his body was saturated would he move on to do the same for his energy cloud.

He went through this same process until he had another epiphany during one of his morning sessions. He had been letting his mind wander as he focused on feeling love. He was slowly allowing it to spread outward, through his limbs and neck, when a simple truth occurred to him: There is no time.

The concept was simple, though he knew many people chose to see it from a perspective outside of quantum physics. Specifically, many people chose to believe time was linear. They believed in a past, a present, and a future. Xander had learned through his studies of quantum physics, however, that the whole concept of time was invented by humans. He believed time was invented for much the same reason as ancient civilizations invented various gods—to explain things they couldn't understand.

The significance of his epiphany was that he did not have to spend a certain amount of time to effectively meditate. He realized he created his sessions out of his belief that his process of filling his body and energy cloud up with love needed to take time. He understood now that he could perform his meditation instantly.

Xander was excited at his revelation, but even more so when he coupled it with his knowing about all energy being one. With this knowledge, he could feel love, fill his body and energy cloud up with its bright blue light, and extend that feeling and energy to the entire universe... and in no time at all.

He stopped his timed sessions but practiced his self-love many times throughout his day until he was doing it more and more often, and without having to stop whatever else he was doing. He still would sit for a few minutes and rotate his attention through his empirical senses, but that was for relaxation and enjoyment.

He and Serenity had not seen each other since the hike, but he had managed to reach her by phone a couple of times, once on the day after Xander had his epiphany. He was quite excited when he shared the information with her, and his voice conveyed his excitement. Although Xander wasn't surprised that Serenity had realized his new lesson years before he did, her enthusiastic response that he had figured it out did not disappoint him. He went on to tell her about his new practice in lieu of the time-conscious sessions he had had, sometimes wasting hours each day.

"There's no such thing as wasting time unless you're dwelling in the past or worrying about the future," she said. "If you're not doing one of those things, you're in the present. Just remember you're doing what you choose to do."

"Well, I just wish I had learned this lesson a long time ago," Xander replied.

Serenity sighed. "You need more practice," she said and then hung up on him.

Xander pulled his cellphone away to look at it.

Had they been disconnected, he wondered, but only for a second. *Yes, by Serenity.*

He thought about what he had said and what she had been able to interpret from his words and from his energy. After thinking about it for a minute, he realized she was right, as usual. It was okay that he was thinking about the past, as long as he wasn't dwelling in it. But, he was being hard on himself for not having learned the lesson sooner and that was not loving himself. He knew that people learned things through realization when they were ready to learn them and not before. He also knew that part of loving himself meant that he was happy with himself as he is now, regardless of what he knows and does not know. He agreed with Serenity. He needed more practice.

CHAPTER 22

Xander had all but stopped attending the unschooling meet-ups. Tracy was growing weaker and was tired most of the time, and Xander was no longer interested since he could drive himself to a park practically any time he wanted. He and David still talked once in a while by phone, but the calls were diminishing in length and frequency. David had met and become friends with a new boy in the group, and Xander could sense David's cloud becoming thinner and brighter and was happy about that.

He wasn't as happy about his progress with helping his mother heal herself, although he continued to try. He found that she responded better to a subtle approach rather than trying to teach her to use her energy directly. He listened closely when she talked and used terms she used when trying to explain things. When she told him how important it was for people to think positively, instead of talking about how her emotions affect her energy, he agreed with her that having a good attitude makes all the difference. He even told her that children usually follow their parents' example when it came to attitude and behavior. Though they agreed, Xander realized his mother was missing a crucial part of the understanding that was key to her healing herself. She thought speaking and behaving positively was the same as having positive feelings, but Xander knew that was not the case at all.

He continued to practice staying in the moment and was surprised whenever he noticed his mother had flipped a page on the monthly calendar that hung on the kitchen wall. It was easy for him since his days were busy taking care of his mom, talking with Serenity, and working at a local grocery store. He had gotten a part-time job despite his mother's pleading for him to consider college instead. She insisted that she could support them both while he went to school, despite the fact that she admitted she believed a college education was overrated but, like money, a necessary evil in society.

Xander told her that he wasn't ready at the moment to go to school, but that he needed, not wanted, money to be able to contribute something to their household since he was nearing adulthood. The job paid minimum wage, but it gave him time to practice his conscious meditations, and he enjoyed seeing and helping people. He had other motivators, though. He wanted a car of his own, and he wanted cash on hand in case Serenity ever agreed to let him take her on an actual date. Serenity hadn't given him a chance to pay for her the time they met at the coffee house or the night they went bowling, and their only other non-phone engagements had been walks and hikes. Even though their dates had never felt like romantic ones, he liked her and was still hopeful future ones would evolve to be so.

Shortly before his eighteenth birthday, Xander was in a back room sweeping at the end of his shift when he heard someone enter through the swinging doors behind him.

"What's this I hear about you turning down a promotion?" said a deep male voice.

Xander stopped sweeping and turned around wearing a grin. He looked back at the two swing-shift stockers, Ray and Helen.

"I heard Joe offered you assistant inventory manager and you turned it down," said Ray.

"Along with a frickin' huge raise," Helen added.

Xander leaned against the push broom, still grinning, and served back, "And along with a frickin' huge amount of responsibility, not to mention double the hours."

"But how can you turn down that pay?" asked Helen.

"Why do I need more money?"

"So you can do what you want."

"But I'm already doing what I want."

That left them speechless.

Xander resumed sweeping, still feeling their stares on his back.

He finished his shift and left the store feeling good about his decision. In fact, he felt good about himself all around. He smiled as he walked to the car, knowing that his practice of loving himself must be working if he was experiencing unreasonable happiness. He felt so good, in fact, that he wished for a challenge to test his new capacity—and the universe granted his wish.

He noticed his aunt Rebecca's car in front of the house when he pulled into the driveway. Once he cut the engine, he reached with his senses to see what mood his aunt and his mother were experiencing, so he would know what not to do that would make things worse. But he didn't sense his mother's energy cloud. He quickened his step toward the house and felt a rush of adrenaline as his aunt opened the door as he reached it.

"What?" asked Xander.

Rebecca held her hands up and said, "Your mother's okay... at the moment."

Xander came to an abrupt stop in front of her.

"I came to check on her when she didn't answer my text or call, and I found her unconscious, so I called 911."

"Why didn't you call me when you couldn't reach her, or at least when you called the ambulance?" Xander asked, feeling anger rise in him.

"I did call you. Several times." Xander kept his phone on vibrate while he was at work and realized he must not have felt it. "Anyway, she woke up before the ambulance even got here, and she's okay. I was just about to call the store and have you paged when I heard you pull in."

Xander had pulled his phone from his pocket and was looking at the three missed calls and two new texts from his aunt.

"Sorry."

"Don't be," replied Rebecca. "Just go get changed and eat something and I'll drive you to the hospital."

"I'm ready to go now."

Rebecca wrapped him in a hug and gave him a quick squeeze and then released him.

"Okay. Let's go."

CHAPTER

Xander tried to block out his mother's energy cloud like a bad smell. Its thick, molasses-like movement reminded him of David's cloud at its nastiest, but this was worse. It was dark brown, with the texture of thick vomit, and blocking it was all Xander could do to prevent himself from vomiting. He had to continue to charge his own cloud whenever he was with her, but even with charging it, it was becoming more difficult to be around her for any length of time.

He sat in a chair beside the hospital bed and held his mother's hand. The doctor had just left the room, with Rebecca right on her heels demanding answers to questions she had about the news the doctor had just shared. Apparently, the cancer had metastasized, and it had been missed during her recent examinations, but Tracy was too weak to undergo further chemo or radiation. The doctor said she should "get her affairs in order," and it was time to talk about options, depending on whether she regained enough strength to go home. It was clear to Xander that his mother was doing her very best to act brave for him, and Xander did his best to return the favor.

"Your aunt Rebecca said you're welcome to stay with her until I come home, but I told her it was up to you," she said, and Xander could hear a slight wheeze in her shallow breaths.

"I'd rather stay at home. It's closer to the hospital and to work. Besides, I want to keep it up and be there in case—for when you come home." They both caught his slip up.

"I told her that's what you'd want to do. Look, honey, don't you worry about me. I just need to rest up, and I'd rather it be a nurse and not you that has to wait on me."

Xander faked a smile and said, "You don't have to worry about me either, Mother."

She returned his squeeze as best she could and started blinking tears. "You've always been able to see the truth in people and in situations," she said, sniffing. "You know I'm not coming home, right?"

Xander nodded, and his own eyes started watering.

It took an effort on her part, but Tracy rolled herself onto her side so she could hold his hand with both of hers.

"I've never been great with money, but I did manage to keep up on my life insurance policy. I took it out right after you were born... probably the only time I listened to my sister."

They both chuckled, and Xander wiped his eyes with the back of his free hand. Then Tracy became stern and pulled his hand to her chest.

"The policy's for a million dollars. You've never asked for much, never needed much, so that should last you quite a while."

Xander was only able to half-listen once he realized his mother was starting to tell him goodbye.

"Just make me one promise. You'll use it to make yourself happy."

Xander already understood that nothing outside himself could make him happy, but he still appreciated the money, and the thought.

"Work, don't work, go to college, don't go to college, it's up to you. Just be sure that whatever you decide to do, you're happy doing it. Don't do something because you think it will make you happy later." She squeezed and yanked his hand, "Promise me!"

Xander smiled for real. "I promise, Mother."

Tracy was in the hospital for six weeks and Xander visited her every day. Despite keeping his energy cloud charged, he became used to the strain of feeling his mother's diseased cloud. Even when he wasn't with her, he would keep his senses directed toward her to detect any changes, and so he felt the exact moment she died.

He was practicing his conscious meditation while stocking some shelves at work, when he had the momentary sensation of near weightlessness. It took him a few seconds to realize what had happened, but the reason was clear when he tried to probe his mother's cloud. He could not sense it at all.

He walked calmly to the manager's office while experiencing both sadness and relief, and he did his best to replace those with feelings of love for his mother. After informing his supervisor of the news, he drove home to change and eat before heading to the hospital to say goodbye. His aunt Rebecca called him crying as he pulled into his driveway. Xander listened to her sobbing as she told him his mother had passed away, and he automatically reached out to sense her energy cloud. Strong waves of anger, fear, sympathy, and self-pity had already formed a thin veil over her cloud, which reminded Xander to recharge his own.

Rebecca arranged and paid for a small funeral so Xander wouldn't have to worry about it. He told her about the money and said he could handle it, but he knew she did not yet think of him as an adult. Several families from the unschooling group attended the funeral, including Chrissy and David. And Serenity was there as well. Xander had charged his cloud, but he was already overwhelmed with his own emotions to keep from being affected by the multiple other clouds that were saturated with unhealthy energy, mostly grief and sorrow.

After the ceremony and the offers of condolences and of help with everything from rides to food, everyone started leaving. Serenity was the last one to approach, and Xander felt ready to receive sympathy from her. With any luck, Xander thought, along with a complementary hug.

"Wanna go on a hike?" she asked.

Xander was put off by her unusual request, given the occasion, and by her not meeting his expectations.

"A hike? Are you serious? My mother just died."

"I know. I attended the funeral."

Xander started to turn away, scoffing and shaking his head.

"Why are you so sad?" she demanded.

Xander turned on her sharply. "Why am I sad? My mother just died!" he yelled at her.

"You said that, but why are you sad?"

Xander was now confused. He could tell she was serious in her question, but didn't understand why she was asking it.

"My mother…" he started to say.

"Yes, I know your mother just died. But tell me why that makes you sad."

Xander thought about the question.

Why does my mother dying make me sad? he asked himself. *Because she's gone and I won't be able to see her or talk with her again. Ever.*

"Because I miss her and I know I won't ever be able to see her again."

Serenity's whole demeanor relaxed. "But why are you sad?"

"I don't under—"

She cut him off again. "I mean, why can't you miss her and still choose to be happy? She'll be dead for the rest of your life, so are you going to be sad for the rest of your life?"

"Of course not," Xander retorted. "I guess I'm mourning. People mourn."

"Yes, you're allowed to mourn and feel sad, angry, lonely, whatever. But remember, Xander, it's up to you how long you choose to feel that way. And don't worry about what other people think."

Xander was tired and didn't want to argue. "What do you mean?" he asked in a surrendering tone.

"You're not happy while you mourn, and you know by now that happiness is a choice and the most important thing there is."

"So..."

"So, however long you mourn, however long you remain unhappy, that's your choice, too. Mourning doesn't bring anyone back from the dead, and it certainly doesn't help you. It only satisfies people who expect you to mourn. The same people who will judge how you do it and for how long you do it."

She took his hands in hers and squeezed them for a second to ensure she had his attention. "Xander, I wouldn't be saying this to just anyone, because most people wouldn't understand. But you're ready to hear it."

Xander knew what she said was true, that the only reason people had to mourn was because it was expected. He could miss his mother and still choose to be happy. After all, he loved her, she was no longer suffering, and he didn't have to be sad about either. He got it.

He felt himself relax a bit and smiled at Serenity. "Thank you."

"No problem. Let me know if you change your mind about that hike."

CHAPTER 34

I T took a few weeks for the insurance money to make its way to Xander, but it eventually did. Since he was now eighteen and a legal adult, he was able to handle the transaction without the help of his aunt Rebecca, though she continued to offer her assistance to him for that and for everything from food shopping to helping him downsize into an apartment. He thanked her each time she offered, but put her off by saying he had to learn to be self-sufficient.

He settled on a one-bedroom apartment between the local college and the grocery store where he worked. As it turned out, it was also a few minutes closer to Serenity's house. Even though he didn't need to work, he kept his stocking job. He liked his job, his new apartment, and spending time with Serenity. In fact, apart from missing his mother, he felt happy most of the time. He also felt like he was starting to truly love himself, but when he told that to Serenity, she responded with, "We'll see."

Xander didn't let her response bother him too much, and he forgot about it soon after, only to be reminded of it a month later when Serenity announced to him she was moving out of state.

"What? When did you decide this?" he demanded.

Serenity remained her calm, collected, indifferent self.

"I've been thinking about it for a while, but I just made the decision last night."

Thoughts and emotions were racing through Xander, overwhelming him. He blinked and stuttered, "Last night? But... what... why didn't..."

She raised an eyebrow at him, "What did you expect?"

Xander recognized he did have expectations. "I don't know... certainly not this!"

"But you had some expectations... and they obviously weren't met."

He felt juvenile in front of her just then and knew that was a sign of not loving himself enough. *Back to basics*, he thought and took a deep, calming breath and filled himself with love. *What did I expect?*

"You just surprised me... and I'm disappointed that you didn't tell me. That I didn't know you were even thinking about going away." He felt better.

"Hmm. I understand you being surprised... but why on earth would you expect me to have told you about going away?"

Xander acted offended. "Because we're friends."

"What... if we don't tell each other everything then we're not friends? And what if I had told you? The only thing that would be different is that you wouldn't be surprised right now."

They were silent for a moment, each thinking about what the other had said. Xander was confused. What she said made sense, as usual, but he still felt disappointed that he hadn't known. He didn't know what else to say that wouldn't make him feel immature.

Damn, he thought. *Here I am again.* He tried to refocus on a bright blue light filling him up.

The awkward silence between them was finally broken by Serenity. "Look, I understand you would have appreciated me... thinking about your feelings."

"Thank you." Xander felt juvenile again.

Serenity shook her head. "You don't get it, Xander."

He looked confused and realized he must not get it.

"I'm not responsible for your feelings. No one is but you. Don't you see? You will always be potentially setting yourself up to get hurt when you have expectations, because you can't control other people. And another thing, don't imagine your own meaning or intentions into what others do."

Xander's confusion was still apparent, so Serenity continued.

"You think the fact that I didn't talk to you about college means that I don't care about you... and that's just not true. I care about you very much," and she grabbed his shoulders and planted a firm kiss right on his lips.

He took hold of her waist and pulled her into him, and kissed her back. All of Xander's thoughts vanished as they were displaced by strong feelings of love.

Serenity let her lips drift away from his and she rested her forehead against his with her eyes closed. "Now, don't assume anything or read into that."

She's reading my mind again, thought Xander, as he had already begun wondering where that kiss would lead.

CHAPTER 35

SERENITY moved a month later. School didn't begin for a couple of months after that, but she wanted to give herself time to get acquainted with the new area and find a job. On Xander's suggestion, they met at the coffee shop on her way out of town. She had agreed, but said it wasn't necessary. *Indifferent to the last,* Xander thought, but he insisted. He didn't tell her he had a going-away gift for her.

Xander was already there when she pulled into the last empty space on the street in front of the shop. He thought her car did not look like the car of a person moving away from home for the first time. He had imagined it would be packed full, with boxes and bags and things piled so high she would have to use her side mirrors to see behind her. He made a note to himself not to tell Serenity about his surprise, since he realized it was merely his assumption and expectation that created that image in his mind.

She came and sat down with a grin when she saw Xander waving her right to the table. He had already bought her a mocha and had staged it on the table across from him, next to a pink gift bag that was lying on its side.

"Just something little for you. I couldn't get it to stay standing up," Xander said in response to her quizzical expression.

She dug into the bag and pulled out a brown leather journal. She ran a hand across it to feel the texture, then opened it up and flipped the pages with her thumb.

"I'm not really into stuff. I don't like clutter."

Xander's heart sank, and he wondered why it was only with Serenity that his feelings seemed to expand beyond his control.

"But this I'll use. Thank you, Xander," she said with a loving smile, to which Xander beamed back one of his own.

After talking and reminiscing about their more interesting hikes, Xander walked her to her car and said goodbye. They hugged and she gave him another kiss on the lips, which he returned with pleasure. They agreed to keep in touch via phone and social media, and Xander said he would come visit her sometime. To his dismay, she only replied with an indifferent-sounding "That'd be great."

He stood on the sidewalk and waved to her as she drove off, hoping she would look back and return his wave, but he saw no sign of either. With a deep sigh, he walked to his own car and drove home, trying to sort through the confusing emotions and thoughts that were reverberating inside of him. He was sure of the truth of Serenity's words about the importance of not making assumptions and having expectations, but he felt conflicted because his emotions seemed to drive the creation of both. Emotions like confusion, frustration, and heartbreak.

Mostly, though, he felt love... love for the friend, the teacher, the woman who had just driven away.

CHAPTER 26

KNOWING that his emotions stemmed from him not fully loving himself, Xander set his mind to do just that. In between sleep, work, and his aunt Rebecca's sporadic checks on his well-being disguised as invitations to dinner, he continued to do his meditations and visualizations, and he researched as much about energy and auras as he could find. After reading studies on auras that seemed to be affected by coming in contact with other energy fields, he decided to try some more experimenting of his own. Though knew he could not directly control another person's energy, and despite not being successful with healing his mother, he believed there was a chance he could still learn how to use energy to help others.

He brainstormed ideas that would allow him to practice working with energy and test his theory. Since he was only working part-time, he decided he still had plenty of hours during the week to volunteer, and volunteer he did. He wasn't able to find a regular volunteer position, but he made do with temporary ones, including cleaning at a community center, serving dinners at a senior center, and doing odd jobs for two churches. Each venue had diverse populations, and each provided him with opportunities to practice using his own energy to help others.

During his time volunteering, he came in contact with people who were physically ill, emotionally troubled, and often both. The people and their energy clouds were as unique as their individual fingerprints, but Xander found one common denominator in them. It was the one thing that all clouds he had ever seen shared, save for the one belonging to Serenity. The energy in all the clouds was unbalanced, some significantly more than others. The ones that had both physical and emotional issues were much more unbalanced than those who had only minor problems. Xander had come to think of a healthy energy cloud as being balanced not when it contained equal parts of healthy and unhealthy energy or all merely one color, but when it *felt* balanced. He couldn't think of any better way to describe it.

He would practice every chance he had, and he had a lot of chances. He started off trying to improve the moods of people he encountered who were depressed or sad or just feeling off for some reason. When he noticed that kind of behavior or demeanor in a person, he would look at the person's energy cloud and try to identify the spot in the cloud where the instigating energy was present. Once he found it, he would form his own energy into the shape of a soft mitten, covering and gently massaging that problem area in the other cloud. Sometimes that worked, and sometimes it didn't. When he needed to be more invasive, his energy would become a broom that he would use to sweep at the unhealthy energy to either thin it out or eliminate it. Once he started seeing some success with those methods, he looked for greater challenges.

When someone would complain to him about a minor ailment, or when he saw someone wince from pain or discomfort, he would perform an examination and, if he was able to identify the energy culprit, try to eradicate or reduce it. As time went on, he had more and more success with helping people feel better and happier. Once he was confident in his new ability, he decided to share the news with Serenity.

She had been gone for three months and had been busy. Too busy, in fact, to talk with Xander as much as he would have liked. He never complained to her, since he knew his disappointment was a result of his own expectations, and Serenity would be sure to point that out to him if he were to say anything. She did respond to his texts fairly regularly, so he sent her one and asked when a convenient time would be for them to catch up. She replied to his text with a one-word message: *Tonight.*

Xander called after dinner and they talked for almost an hour. Xander contained his excitement about his success while he listened to Serenity tell him about her classes and new friends. He felt a pang of jealousy when she mentioned one particular person, Richard, more than once, but quickly recognized his thinking error and brought himself back to the moment and focused on listening.

After she had finished, she asked Xander what was new with him, and he didn't hesitate for a second to tell her about his energy experiments. He spoke in detail to her, since she was the only one he knew who would understand what he had been doing. Once he had finished, he paused and awaited her validation of the pride he was feeling over his success.

"That's very interesting," was all she said at first.

"Interesting? That's all you have to say?" Xander said, not hiding his disappointment. He caught himself again and added, "Oops... there go my expectations again."

"Good catch," she said. "I'm actually pretty impressed, both at what you say you were able to do and at your intentions. But my interest is in the moral implications of you doing what you did to those people without their permission."

"But I was helping them," Xander said in defense.

"I agree, but you wouldn't force feed someone cold medicine or an antidepressant, would you?"

Xander thought about that, trying to swallow his pride and restrain his ego. He wanted to argue with her, convince her what he did was right.

"Serenity, it's not like I was doing something that could hurt them. On the contrary, it was for their own good."

He didn't want to push too hard, just enough that she would see his side and validate the good he was doing, but the silence was almost painful. He was wondering if he had already overdone it, but waited to break the quiet until he felt he could not wait any longer.

Just as he was about to back pedal, Serenity spoke up. "Xander, I know you didn't mean any harm, but you're interfering in people's lives. Unless they ask for or willingly accept your help, you may do more harm than good. Trust me, I know."

Questions competed in Xander's mind to be the first to spring from his mouth, so he asked none. In fact, he didn't say a thing for almost a minute. He had never heard Serenity speak with so much passion and desperately wished he was with her in person to see that passion on her face. He wanted to stare her in the face and ask her what it mattered whether someone knew he was helping them and what harm she thought he could do to someone simply by trying to balance their energy. The question that he wanted to know more than the others, and the question that won out over the others in the competition, shot out of his mouth before he could even think to stop it.

"What do you mean, you know?"

The silence on the other end of the line continued for several seconds. The other questions in Xander's head had disappeared for the moment, replaced by new ones, as he tried to imagine what she could possibly have meant.

Did she know how to balance or manipulate other people's energy? For what reason? Had she been successful in healing people? And then a dark thought appeared. *What had gone wrong?*

"I'm not going to talk about that right now," she said.

As direct as ever, Xander thought. "You brought it up. I just want to know if…"

"Xander. Did you not hear me? I said I'm not going to talk about that right now."

"Okay, okay," Xander said, disappointed, hoping he had not already shortened the life span of their current conversation, but knowing he probably had.

"I'm going to go now," she said, and waited for his response. When none came, she added, "Look, I'm tired, and when I'm tired I'm off balance. Someday, I'll tell you about… some things in my past, but when I'm ready. I promise you… and I don't usually make promises."

Xander's own emotions were threatening to overwhelm him. He was intrigued about Serenity's past, frustrated that she would not share it with him, and excited and hopeful that she made him a promise… something she never did.

He swallowed hard and said, "Okay, I understand."

"Thank you. I'll talk to you soon. Good night," she said, and hung up without waiting for a response.

Xander tried to watch a documentary, but he turned it off when he realized he was staring through the screen and not paying attention to the program. He went to bed early and tried to read, but experienced nearly the same phenomenon with his quantum physics book. Seeing the futility of distracting himself, he turned off the light and stared up into the darkness.

After what seemed like hours, he finally fell to sleep. His last conscious thought was the same one that had been reverberating in his head since he had hung up the phone—*What had Serenity meant when she said, "trust me, I know"?*

CHAPTER 37

As months passed, Xander's anticipation to learn Serenity's secret grew. She had promised to tell him when she was ready, but Xander didn't know when that would be any better than he knew the secret itself. They hadn't spoken since their phone conversation due to abstract busyness, and Xander did his best not to read into it. Since then, he had thought a lot about what she had dubbed as "the moral implications" of his using his energy on other people's clouds without their knowledge and permission. Despite his attempt to rationalize his actions, he knew the truth of what she had said. He had played out scenarios in his head in which he tried to obtain permission to help people with their energy clouds, but they inevitably ended with strange looks, laughter, or both. Since he had no intention of walking up to a person, especially a stranger, and asking that, he decided not to continue his practice unless there was an emergency that warranted his intervention.

He stopped volunteering at the senior and community centers but continued his volunteer work with the churches because the energy was more positive in that environment and he was happy doing it. He also continued practicing his self-love exercises, and he meditated often. When he meditated, he sometimes would ask himself a question before beginning his deep breathing. Lately, he had been repeatedly asking the same question: *Why am I so affected by Serenity?* After asking it, he would focus on his breathing, direct his attention to rotate through his senses, and try not to think about the question. He was only able to let the question fade from his mind during his meditations because he spent so much time thinking about it at nights while he tried to fall asleep.

The short answer was that he was in love with her. Unfortunately, that didn't explain why he was so quick to become overwhelmed with emotions, so much so that they seemed to change his thinking and behavior before he realized it. After all, he had loved before. Of course, that had been the platonic love of his mother, his aunt, and even, in a strange way, David. However, he and Serenity had kissed, and he knew their love for each other was on a different level than the others, and he knew the kiss alone was not the source of their love.

We never said out loud that we love each other, Xander thought.

He wasn't afraid to tell her, but he was afraid of how she would respond. He did believe she loved him, but he knew better than to trust that her response would meet his expectations, regardless of how she felt about him.

"It all comes back to self-love," he said aloud to himself one night.

It was late and he had been lying awake, staring at the dark and then at the ceiling once his eyes had adjusted. He had just remembered something that Serenity had told him.

"Do you know what causes the most problems with people? What people do to dirty and stain their own auras more than anything?" she had asked, and then answered, *"People don't love themselves."*

Of course, that was the answer. He loved her, and he felt he needed her, but that same conditional love and need were proof that he did not feel complete without her, did not love himself. He also realized the paradox of his situation—that Serenity would never be with him in the way he wanted unless he learned to love himself, until he freed himself from his attachments and from his expectations... until he didn't need her or anyone... until he could love her regardless of whether she was with him or even whether she loved him back. The only chance he had of being with her was to be happy with himself regardless of whether they would ever be together.

It finally made sense to him. This is what Serenity had been trying to tell him—what she herself did.

All I need to do is be happy with me, he thought, *that's all anyone needs to do... and it's just a matter of making that choice.*

Smiling, he closed his eyes and fell asleep, feeling better than he had in a long time.

CHAPTER

XANDER found that the more he was able to love himself, the happier he was with everything in his life. He also learned that the more choices he made that made him happy, the more he was able to love himself. It made sense to him, though he thought it strange at first. He started with his thoughts about himself, ensuring they were consistently positive ones. He didn't have to exaggerate, but merely acknowledge positive things. When he looked in the mirror, he made himself smile and tell himself he liked who he was, inside and out. When he made a decision, he did his best to detach from the outcome and then latched on to a good feeling about his decision. He looked objectively at everything in his life and, if he wasn't happy doing it, he either stopped doing it or, if he saw some benefit in continuing to do it, he changed his perspective about that thing so he felt good doing it.

He also continued working with and learning about his energy cloud, and he became quite proficient at changing its size, shape, and movement. Charging it was also now second nature to him, and he got to the point where he would do it without thinking about it. He would just picture and feel pure white energy surging into him from above him while bright green energy flooded him from the ground. That also helped him continue to feel good about himself and love himself more and more each day, and in the healthiest way.

He also kept his job and, after much pleading from his supervisor, accepted more hours. Xander agreed to the offer after considering it overnight, during which he decided he did enjoy the time he spent at the store, and the extra hours would allow him to sustain his current lifestyle without touching his inheritance. His coworkers were as pleased with his decision as their supervisor, though both joked about him choosing to stay in such a lousy job.

"But I thought you didn't do drugs," Ray joked.

"I don't. I'm just high on life!" Xander joked back.

Ray and Helen just shook their heads at him.

"Maybe you need to start taking drugs," Helen said, walking away.

Xander knew they didn't understand or agree with his priorities, but that was their issue, and it couldn't affect him unless he let it. Anyway, they were a big part of why he enjoyed his job enough to stay there and to increase his hours.

Toward the end of one shift, Xander was kneeling down next to his cart and stocking cans on a shelf when someone tapped the back of his head, tilting his ball cap over his eyes. He turned his head and saw Helen looking back at him while continuing down the aisle.

"I'm going to straighten up the back room, X-man,"

"Okay." Xander answered, fixing his hat. He continued to watch Helen walk away, sensing something odd. He focused on her cloud and noticed a strange tint to a section near the lower perimeter. He reached out with his senses and felt a sickly sensation associated with the tinge. Returning to his stocking, he finished emptying the boxes and pushed the cart to the back room. After stowing the cart, he looked for Helen and found her sitting on a couple of stacked boxes, slumped back against the wall with her eyes closed.

"Helen?" he asked and hurried toward her.

He could tell something was wrong because her lower jaw was slack and hanging to the side. She didn't respond, and Xander grabbed her shoulders and called her name again. He also began charging his energy, but only realized he was doing it when he felt and then saw the bright light rushing through his arms and straight into Helen.

He was transfixed as he watched the energy course through his cloud and into hers, heading directly to the sickly tinge and smothering it until it was gone. The event lasted only seconds, but that was enough. Helen's eyelids fluttered open. She sat up straighter on the boxes, grabbing Xander's arms to balance herself.

"Are you okay?" Xander asked.

She was still disoriented. She looked around the room and finally recognized Xander. "Yeah. I'm fine. Thanks."

Xander released her shoulders and sat down next to her, wondering whether she would collapse again. He felt an internal nudge to ask her a question, and he followed it.

"Are you diabetic or anemic?"

Helen dropped her head and grinned.

"You could say I'm anemic. I'm on my period."

Xander wasn't embarrassed, but Helen must have assumed he was and added, "It's no big deal. I have a heavy flow. Plus, I was out late last night and I've barely eaten anything. This is not the first time I've done this to myself."

She stood up, and Xander knew by her cloud she felt better.

"Anyway, I feel better. I'm going to go clock out. See you."

On his short drive home, Xander thought about the discoveries he had made and the excitement of his thoughts kept him from falling asleep for a while... again.

He realized his ability to charge his energy cloud so quickly and without thinking about it was handy. He also learned that physical contact seemed to enhance the effect of one cloud over another. In this case, his touching Helen's shoulders while his cloud was charging easily pushed the weak, sickly energy from her cloud. He was especially excited to receive a nudge that turned out to be right. His only guess as to how that happened was that he had somehow received the information from Helen herself. He suddenly remembered his quantum physics and it dawned on him that all energy is connected, so he technically had access to that information.

His conversation with Serenity regarding morality popped into his head, but he told himself that his action was not premeditated and happened in the moment, so he did not view it as a violation of Helen's rights. He had learned this ability, so it must serve a purpose. If he could not use it on a daily basis to help people with regular issues, then emergency issues must be a just reason to use it.

The image of the sickly tinge in Helen's cloud appeared in his mind. The feeling more than the color somehow reminded him of David, and that memory changed to that of his mother.

If only I had known all this when she was still alive, he thought.

He recognized the negativity that had sneaked into his consciousness and stopped it with a sly grin. *Oh, no you don't*, he said silently to the self-pity, guilt, and ego that had tried to mount an insurrection. *I happen to love me and my ability*, he thought. And he meant it, too.

Before falling off to sleep, he felt gratitude for the many wonderful things in his life, including and especially his new ability. He wondered if he would ever have a call to use it again and, if so, how soon. Once again, the universe answered him.

CHAPTER 39

THE next morning, Xander was enjoying a walk on the campus of the local college. He didn't attend classes there, but the school was close to his apartment and was beautifully landscaped. He remembered feeling the warmth of the sun each time the cool breeze stopped. He could hear people, birds, and the traffic, and he listened to the concert of raking, weed-eating, and a distant lawnmower. There were people everywhere, sitting and playing on the grass, jogging and riding bikes, and walking. A couple walked toward him on the sidewalk, their individual energy clouds moving smoothly, easily blending into a harmonious cloud around them. The man's own energy had a tan tint to it and felt a little off to Xander, but he sensed nothing specific. Their love for each other was clear and Xander noticed they weren't speaking, simply smiling, holding hands and enjoying each other as they walked. He looked away and smiled himself, also enjoying their combined, positive contribution to the world in the moment as they passed by him. A few steps later, he suddenly felt an internal nudge and glanced back at them. They had stopped, and the woman was turned to the man, who was wobbling. Xander could see that the man's tan energy had changed to a dark brown. His knees buckled and his body crumpled sideways. Luckily for him, he fell so his head and face hit the grass instead of the concrete.

Xander didn't remember making a conscious choice about it, but he found himself quickly moving toward the couple even before the woman started screaming. He didn't remember actually thinking of what he was doing, but he knelt beside the man and rolled him over onto his back.

Xander could see the eye of the storm in the man's energy cloud, a dark brown swirling soup above where his heart. He suddenly experienced déjà vu as he thought about the times in the past when he had seen this type of energy. It was never good.

Xander placed one of his hands on the man's chest and the other on the grass. He began visualizing a surge of energy, pure white, coming down from the sky and through his own body into the ground. Then he envisioned healing energy, a light green light, coming up from the earth through his hand, up his arm, across his chest, and down through his other arm into the man. He pictured the green energy saturating the man's chest and mixing with the brown energy that was surrounding his heart.

He saw the healing energy from the earth steadily dilute the brown energy, slowing and eventually stopping the swirling. After a minute or so, the brown soup disappeared entirely.

He's lucky I learned to charge my energy while helping others, Xander thought, and briefly thought of his mother.

Xander watched the lines in the man's face soften and his body relax as the pain gradually dissolved. One by one, Xander became aware of his own senses again. He could hear the man's breathing deepen, becoming audible despite the murmuring of the crowd that had formed around them. Feeling the balance restored to the energy and heartbeat beneath his hand, he settled back and looked up to meet the eyes of the curious people who had gathered to watch. He sensed a mix of energies surrounding him— confusion, skepticism, relief, awe, and disbelief. He could only imagine the thoughts of the spectators, but he had learned from Serenity to understand people by reading their energy. Of course, he could have guessed based on the looks on their faces. The thoughts were not anything unusual. They would be the typical ones.

What just happened? Oh my God! I don't believe it!

Then he heard actual voices.

"Holy shit!" exclaimed a young man who looked like he could still be in high school. "Did you just save his life?"

A woman who looked to be in her early twenties took a step forward and asked excitedly, "What did you do?"

A few other people had approached. Xander knew because one of them exclaimed, "That's not how you do CPR!"

The questions paused as the crowd awaited a response to satisfy their individual, internal questions and, in most cases, he knew, to judge him.

"I just helped him balance his energy," he said to the woman who had asked the question.

The man's companion was sobbing and hugging the man, who had opened his eyes, but was obviously disoriented. Without breaking her hug, she turned her head toward Xander and mouthed, *thank you*. He nodded to her and stood up amidst that feeling of various spikes of energy, which he had come to understand were associated with sadness, relief, bewilderment, and anger.

That's okay. We all feel, Xander reminded himself.

He chose not to linger in that moment now that it had passed and, ignoring the various comments and the approaching sirens, walked on with a continued appreciation for the world around him.

CHAPTER 40

XANDER eventually found himself back at his apartment. It was a simple place, which is why he liked it. It had one bedroom, a galley kitchen, and a small living room with more than enough room for a loveseat, a small coffee table, one comfortable chair, and an end table made from stacked plastic totes. The one window in the living room looked out over the street. That worked well for him, as he tended to sit next to it while he meditated, or he would set his tea on the sill and observe the world. He really enjoyed simple. He found that life was so much easier to appreciate and enjoy when there was less to think about.

He made himself some dandelion tea, sat down on the loveseat, and opened his laptop on the coffee table in front of him. He had decided to start a journal about the things he had learned in life, from his own experiences and from Serenity. He wondered how to begin. *How do other people keep a journal?*, he thought, but he knew he tended to think and see things from a different perspective than most people. Based on what he knew, the things he could do and had done, he thought it was safe to say he thought differently than most people on the planet... although, he thought, that wouldn't be the case forever.

He followed an internal nudge and wrote his journal entries as if he were writing to Serenity, not that he had any specific plans of sharing it with her. At first, he wasn't sure how to start it. Then he recalled a saying he had once heard that seemed appropriate and, while picturing Serenity's face, began a monologue in his mind.

I've heard it said that a fish doesn't know it's wet. I guess that's the best way to explain me. I don't know how I know what I know, and I certainly don't have all the answers. What I do know is that it's okay that I'm different. You and I both know that nothing can make people understand something they're not ready for, but for those who are ready to hear what I have to say, then I suppose they will.

I have never quite understood why people, mostly adults, are so afraid, so often, and of so many things. I have never seen any good come from my being afraid, especially after I learned I could choose to feel something else. That's not to say I've never been afraid, because I have, like when I learned my mother was going to die. But even the few times when I found myself afraid, including my encounters with unhealthy energy, I was able to choose to feel a different emotion once I realized the fear was stopping me from doing anything. Perhaps I wasn't able to change right away, but I did as soon as I recognized that I would rather feel something different.

Back in the earlier days of my life, before I met you, nobody seemed to understand me. I could see you sensed that I was different, and I appreciated that you never tried to force me into any of the societal molds we've often discussed. I also appreciated that you weren't afraid of me and, more importantly, that you didn't ignore me like many other people have done, despite my... quirks.

I remember I was a quiet child. That's probably an understatement, since I started talking when I was four, which was late, at least according to society's expectations. I already knew how, mind you, I just didn't see the point. I saw more value in asking myself questions and then taking action to experience the answers. I was a miniature scientist. When I questioned something to myself, I would start an experiment. I would hypothesize, test theories, and produce findings. If I saw a new toy or an unfamiliar piece of furniture, I would look at it first without attempting to touch it. I would imagine what it would feel like to touch, how heavy it would be to move, if it had a smell to it, if it would make any sound, and what it could become. After my observation, I would begin testing my hypothesis by touching and playing with the object.

Since I wasn't used to using words yet, my thoughts often consisted of feelings and imagined sensory perception. When I was imagining feeling one of the legs of a new school chair, I would imagine the feeling of the cold metal and wouldn't be thinking about any words. I guess I chose not to speak because I didn't want to hear an answer and just think about it. I would rather learn it using my senses. Living in the truest sense of the word is experiencing, not thinking.

My mother didn't seem to mind that I didn't talk much, even if she didn't really understand me. It didn't stop her from talking to me, and her voice was a magical instrument. It didn't seem to matter what she was saying; I always enjoyed listening to it. She was a teacher to me, but she treated me like an equal and not as a subordinate child whether she was teaching me something, telling me about her day, or enforcing a rule for my own safety. I distinctly remember the time she stopped me from exploring an electrical outlet with a paperclip. She swooped in like a superhero and stopped me, and I could sense her fear, but once she knew I was safe she explained the dangerous outcome with a calm voice. I have to say her lesson was rather unique, but it got the point across to me. I remember her showing me a cord to a lamp that was plugged in nearby. She pointed her finger and traced the cord to the lamp and the lamp to the energized bulb. Though I don't remember the full explanation, I got the gist when she explained it was hot and held my tiny finger close enough to feel the radiating heat, and then told me the outlet also was hot. Of course I immediately grasped her message, just as she knew I would.

Xander's mind shifted back to the present, and he realized he had just been staring through the screen of his laptop that was sitting idly on the coffee table in front of him. He knew he had been sitting there for a while, yet realized he hadn't even turned it on. *Oh, well,* he thought, and quickly pushed away the feeling of frustration and regret for wasting time, so as not to waste more. He finished his tea and stood up to put the cup in the sink when a tone coming from the front pocket of his jeans alerted him to a text message. He sighed as he pulled out his smartphone, the one true time-suck from which he had not yet chosen to liberate himself.

The text read, *Wyd?* He started to send a reply, but an incoming call from the same number interrupted him.

"Hey, Paul." He answered.

"Yo."

He instantly recognized his friend's baritone voice, along with chewing noises. Xander smiled as he pictured Paul's lanky frame lying on his couch, his legs splayed over one end, his cellphone in one hand while his other excavated the bag of chips or pretzels Xander could hear in the background.

"Discover any more secrets to the universe?"

"No. I was just chilling," Xander replied, his vernacular adapting to his audience.

"No you weren't. I'm chillin'… you're meditating. There's a difference."

Xander couldn't help but chuckle aloud. He always enjoyed Paul's sense of humor and quick wit, and the day they first met flashed through Xander's mind.

The very funny circumstances surrounding his first encounter with Paul were merely the first in what would become a relatively consistent stream of sarcasm and clever dialogue, at least on Paul's end, which rarely failed to amuse Xander. Paul never laughed at his own humorous actions or words and, perhaps, just wasn't as easily entertained as Xander.

Xander had just returned to his car from the grocery store, had plopped the two plastic bags half-filled with fresh produce, oatmeal, and raw nuts on the passenger seat, and had laid his head back. He closed his eyes, soaked in the warmth from the sun and enjoyed a brief meditation. It was pretty much a sauna. The outside temperature was easily in the mid-eighties, so the car was a great deal hotter. While everyone else he knew kept a door open or immediately opened a window to allow the oven-like heat to escape, Xander had always found it comforting to sit for a few moments in what it must feel like to be wrapped in a damp electric blanket.

A rap on the window snapped him out of his meditation, and he turned his head to see a tall, wiry young man with longish, sandy blond hair pulled into a sloppy ponytail. The man hunched toward the window and stared at Xander with his head cocked, a choppy attempt at a beard on his face.

"You okay, man? You know, there are easier ways to off yourself. Baking yourself… that's a new one on me." He had a deep voice that didn't seem to fit his thin frame.

Xander turned the key and lowered the window. The young man straightened up but retained the expressionless look on his face.

"Uh… yeah. Thanks," Xander said. "I was just meditating."

He caught too late that he should have left off the last part of his response; the man's lopsided grin validated that thought. Xander sat upright and fastened his seat belt.

"Sorry to bring you back to your body. You just looked so… at peace. I thought you might be, you know, resting in peace."

It was Xander's turn to grin. "Thanks. I appreciate the thought."

"No problem. Ciao, dude."

Xander watched him walk away for a few seconds in his untucked, button-up, too-big jeans and even Birkenstocks. Surrounding him was a light blue band of energy that Xander had come to associate with feelings of contentment. He was obviously comfortable with himself and his life.

Xander started up his car and drove to one of his favorite tea bars a couple of miles away. He was people watching and sipping an in-house cup of one of the establishment's creative concoctions, called Dragonheart, when the door tone sounded and the same wiry fellow walked in. It was clear from the sweaty sheen on his face that he had walked from the store. He caught sight of Xander almost at once, grinned his lopsided grin again, walked straight toward him, and sat down across the small table from him.

"We're obviously destined to meet, but you could've offered me a ride. Paul," he said, reaching his long arm and large, open hand across the table.

Xander shook Paul's oversized hand. "Xander. Pleased to meet you, Paul. I didn't want to deprive you of this gorgeous weather. We don't often have this much sun at this time of the year."

His grin was gone, but his eyes still smiled. They almost always did.

"Oh, it's not the sun I mind. It's the walking. I've seen too many injuries from exercise."

Xander smiled back.

That was the first of many wonderful times spent with Paul. On most occasions, Xander drove.

"Okay, you got me, Paul. What's up?"

"Wanna go check out that new action flick tonight? The one where the ancient dudes are fighting each other? It looks like it's Star Wars meets Stargate. Probably too much CGI, and the writing's probably crap, but the action looks good."

Xander hesitated. He usually preferred to watch movies with strong dialogue, but he was also pretty easily entertained. Plus, he thought, there will be a lot of people there to watch. That was always worth it for Xander.

"Sure. What time's it playing?"

"It starts at seven. You can pick me up at six-twenty. Oh... can you drive?"

CHAPTER 44

THEY arrived at the mall in plenty of time for the showing. Rather than even attempting to find a space up front, Xander drove to the end of an aisle and pulled into one of the last parking spots.

"You're trying to force me to exercise, aren't you?" Paul asked with a small whine and a dejected look. "You know you could've found a closer spot. You always do when you want to."

"The weather's beautiful! I just didn't want to deprive you of your only chance to enjoy some this week."

"How do you do that, by the way?" Paul asked sincerely. "Find a spot up front, I mean." He shut the car door and waited with his head cocked for an answer.

"I don't think about how. I just expect a space to be waiting there for me. I… allow it to happen, I guess."

Paul walked around the car shaking his head. "Whatever. Keep your secrets."

Xander loved the mall—or rather, the gathering of people—for different reasons. He looked around and saw so many people strolling, weaving past others, talking, eating, living, loving. He consciously shifted his perspective and looked at the energy clouds enveloping them. Each cloud appeared as unique as each individual it enveloped. So many, yet no one color combination, size, or feel was a twin.

They waited in a short line to buy their tickets and entered the theater only to stand in line again at the concession stand. *It's okay*, thought Xander. Waiting was a wonderful opportunity to observe the world around him. Paul ordered a small popcorn, a soda, and several teaspoons of sugar made to look like some fruit candy. Xander ordered a water and indulged in a bit of sugar for himself. Chocolate-covered peanuts were his one dietary vice when seeing a movie, and he rationalized buying them while making a mental note to balance himself out later with some extra dandelion tea. Paul offered to pay for the snacks, but Xander reached for his wallet even before Paul let it be known that he accidentally left the rest of his cash at home.

"I got it." Xander didn't mind, and neither did Paul.

Xander grinned. He liked the fact that Paul didn't feel guilty about mooching. No pleading a future reciprocation or dramatizing the incident. It was done, and they both moved on with no drama. Xander liked simple.

Sitting in the theater, Paul watched the pre-preview entertainment while Xander took advantage of the additional opportunity to people watch. The lights were still on, so he could see the individual audience members and their energy clouds. Of course, even when the lights were dimmed and finally out, he knew he would still be able to feel their energy clouds as clearly as he could see them with the lights on. He slowly scanned the crowd and recognized the differences in the colors, sizes, shapes, densities, and vibrations of the clouds.

He spotted a couple snuggling up to each other. The man, who could be in his early thirties, clearly kept his physical body fit by exercising and probably by sticking to a relatively healthy diet. However, his cloud was a dark green with red swirls and sparks of brown. Xander associated this combination with stress and anger. Although the man appeared to be enjoying the moment with his wife or girlfriend, his thoughts were usually serious and focused on work or some other worries. Interestingly enough, the recipient of his snuggling had a bright, light green base mixed with soft pink tones. She was also slender but didn't look overly toned. Regardless, Xander knew she was the healthier one in all ways. She was most likely an optimist and didn't take life or herself too seriously. Xander thought perhaps that's why the man was attracted to her.

Looking around at the other clouds, Xander was reminded of his first childhood experiences with energy clouds. The faint glow of the spider that met its demise when it met the sole of his teacher's shoe back in preschool was his first memory of anything of the kind. He also remembered his mother, about how he knew before she did when she started getting sick.

"Holy shit! Did you see that?" Paul said in a loud whisper as he elbowed Xander.

Xander's consciousness shifted back to the present, and he realized the movie had already started.

"Yeah. Wow," he replied. It was obvious by Paul's disappointed smirk that he knew Xander hadn't been paying attention. Paul just shook his head and resumed watching the movie.

Xander dropped Paul back off at his apartment after the movie. As Paul shut the car door, he turned away with a "see you" but without so much as a thanks. Xander didn't expect one from him and noticed only because of the system norms. After all, Xander knew he had had a choice whether or not to take him and to pay for the snacks. He loved that Paul was not interested in conforming.

Back at his apartment, Xander made another cup of tea—jasmine this time—and sat back down on the couch. He turned on his computer and stared at the screen once more. He still didn't know how to start, so he just began typing his thoughts.

"Do I really think differently?" is one question I've never had to ask myself. I have been constantly reminded that I do for as long as I can remember, by my mother and just about everybody else in my life. I was labeled and told as early as kindergarten, before my mom started to homeschool me, which is even before she decided to unschool me (I'm not the only one who thinks differently). My teachers were not as patient with me as either they or I would have liked, and my early mastery of the question "why?" along with seemingly endless follow-up questions definitely warranted patience. Despite the fact that I wasn't asking why just to hear myself talk, they didn't seem interested in teaching anything but what the specific curriculum called for. They had no desire to explain why I had to practice sounding out my letters with the class when I could already read fluently, why we were learning to count pictures of fruit, or why we couldn't ask about anything other than what they were specifically talking about at the time. I once tried to ask one of my teachers a question during recess, guessing that she didn't want to take class time to answer my questions. Her cloud colors immediately changed to a combination I had learned meant she was feeling irritated, and she responded with, "Oh, Xander, just go and play with the others. You don't have to try to be different all the time." Try to be different? I wasn't trying to be anything. I was just being me.

CHAPTER 42

SERENITY had disappeared. She had stopped returning Xander's texts, and when he called her, the recorded message indicated the number had been reassigned. He knew she didn't spend time on social media, and he had never asked for her e-mail. He knew the city and could probably locate her, but as much as he loved her and knew that she loved him, he knew it was not right to chase her. He knew that if their relationship was a priority for them, they would not have lost touch. She was just gone, at least for now, but Xander had learned to love himself enough to be okay with that.

In fact, Xander was okay with everything in his life. More than okay, he was happy. Everything had changed when he started to love himself for everything he was. He knew he couldn't love himself conditionally and that, as he practiced, he had to love every aspect of himself and at all times. That meant he had to love himself when he was working with an energy cloud and when he made a mistake, when he felt confident and when he was sick, and even when he was in love, and the love of his life would take her time to return his texts or calls and then vanish from his life without a word. Loving himself meant he would always be okay, and that made him happy.

Paul, on the other hand, was not okay. Xander noticed a gradual change in his behavior that seemed to coincide with a seriousness not normally seen in Paul. The first sign of anything different was on a weekend. Xander was not working and decided to browse the bookstore. After spending an hour or so skimming through some new books and deciding not to purchase anything, he headed home. On the way, he had a sudden impulse to grab a fruit drink and stopped at a smoothie bar not far from his apartment. There were a few people lined up in front of him, so he had time to look up at the menu posted above the counter. He was still reading it and deciding when he heard a familiar voice.

"How did you know I worked here?" Paul was standing on the other side of the counter wearing a colorful smock and a visor, and a hairnet had captured his ponytail.

"I didn't," Xander said, surprised. "How long have you…"

"I just started yesterday," Paul answered, looking a little sheepish. "What'll you have?"

"Oh, I'll just have the special," Xander said, pointing to the advertisement on the menu above them. Paul rang up the order and Xander paid.

"I'm on break in a few if you want to wait," Paul said, handing Xander his receipt. "I got something to tell you," he added with a smile.

"Sure."

Xander sat at an open table and took small sips of his smoothie while waiting for Paul. He was intrigued by what else he would learn about his friend today. Paul emerged from the back on time and sat down across from Xander.

"I have a girlfriend!" he said before Xander had a chance to ask what he wanted to tell him. He smiled more than Xander had ever seen from him before, and Xander noticed that his mood had improved dramatically since they had stood across the counter from each other.

"Oh… wow," Xander said. He was quite surprised at the news and at Paul's current demeanor. "Is that sudden? I didn't even know you were dating anyone."

"Yeah, it all happened pretty quick. But it's awesome and I couldn't be happier."

Xander was still getting over his surprise, but he felt a strange nudge from what Paul had just said. He took a quick glance at Paul's energy cloud and felt for it with his own. Nothing peculiar stood out to him, though the strange feeling remained.

It's probably just that I haven't known Paul when he's been in a relationship, Xander thought. "So, tell me about her," Xander said and Paul answered as if he had been waiting for Xander's permission.

"Her name's Allison and she's amazing," he began. "She's beautiful, funny, shorter than me, she's going to school to be a nurse... and she likes me!"

Xander couldn't help but chuckle at Paul's animated gestures. "What's not to like?" he teased.

"I know, right? The other girls I've dated were just too engrained in the system to appreciate me... but not my Alli."

"I'm happy for you, Paul, and I'm glad you're happy. You deserve it."

"Thanks, X-man."

"So, how do you like the job so far?" Xander asked. Paul's smile noticeably degraded.

"It's okay. It's a job, you know?"

Xander asked the question that seemed obvious to him: "Then why do it?"

Paul's smile disappeared altogether.

"I can't live in a studio forever, man, and I need a car. Plus, I want to have some cash... for going places."

For going places with Allison, you mean. Xander could see that Paul's priorities had changed. Before Allison, he walked almost everywhere or took the bus. He never seemed to have money on him, but it never bothered him enough to have any more than his parents gave him. Of course, Xander knew that having feelings for someone else can change things. He just hoped his friend would not fall victim to the common scenario of focusing so much on making someone else happy that he lost himself and his happiness in the process.

"Well, break's over. Good seeing you, man," said Paul as they both stood.

"You, too."

Paul nodded and turned away.

"Hey, Paul."

Paul swiveled back around.

"Congrats. I can't wait to meet her," Xander said with a smile.

Paul nodded, smiled, and continued on his way. Xander watched Paul's cloud as he disappeared into the back. He still didn't see anything odd, but he continued to have a strange feeling. Paul looked happy. He was smiling, had a new job and a new girlfriend, but the nudge Xander had was that his friend's happiness was not authentic. He seemed happy on the surface, but Xander wasn't convinced. Paul seemed like he was following a procedure, going through motions that he thought he needed to do to make himself happy. The last time Xander had seen him, he was free-spirited and free-thinking. Now he had a job he didn't really want in order to make money he hadn't needed before in order to please someone other than himself. Xander saw it clearly for what it was—Allison might not be tainted by it, but Paul was getting caught up in the system.

CHAPTER

For days, Xander thought about Paul and his recent choices. The situation reminded him of his mother and some of the things he used to hear her say. One particular conversation between his mother and his aunt Rebecca came to mind.

The conversation had taken place well before his mother was sick, so Rebecca was still being her stern, stubborn self to her younger sister. They had just returned from shopping at a department store and were sitting down on the couch to continue arguing, but this time they had both armed themselves with a glass of wine. Xander sat next to his mother on the corner of the couch and was sitting against some pillows, reading, so he couldn't help but overhear their debate regarding whether his mother should look for a better-paying job.

"All I'm saying is that you two could be doing a lot better if you had a regular, full-time job," Rebecca said. She had calmed down since Tracy had put the wine glass in her hand.

"I have a full-time job," Tracy answered.

"I said a *regular* full-time job. You will never be paid as much working virtually as you would be working in an office environment."

They were both speaking quieter than they had been in the car, but neither would back down from their individual positions.

"You're probably right about that, but besides more money, what else would that mean?"

Rebecca stared at her sister like she was speaking an alien tongue. "What else would that mean? Uh, more money means more money. A better place to live, better clothes, a better car, better food… and a better education for my nephew!"

Tracy would not be daunted. She took a slow, deliberate sip of her wine and placed it on the coffee table.

"You're right. About all of those things, you're right." She paused, allowing her sister to feel the tiniest taste of victory before continuing. "But… it would also mean that I would not be available for Xander for most of the day, every day during the week. It would mean he would be with strangers who don't understand him… people who would treat him like just another sheep. I'm not going to abandon him into the system."

"Oh, Tracy, you're paranoid. You and I were both raised in this system of yours and we turned out okay." Rebecca stated.

"Apparently not… apparently, I don't make enough money."

"Now you're just being childish."

Tracy took another sip of her wine, returned the glass to the table again, and turned sideways on the couch to face her sister head-on. When she spoke, she started out lower and slower.

"Rebecca. Listen closely. Xander is special, you know he is, but even if he wasn't, I would not subject him to whole weeks of… molding to make him another generic citizen. If I can help it, he will grow up knowing he does not have to follow society's checklist."

Rebecca wrinkled her face in annoyance. "Checklist? What checklist?"

Tracy's volume and emotions began to escalate. "Go to school to learn what society says is important. Get a job. Get a loan. Go to college. Get a higher-paying job. Accumulate more debt. Get a job that pays even more. Buy more stuff. Buy bigger stuff. Get a mortgage. Work until you physically can't work anymore. Retire and work some more to continue to pay your debt. Oh… and *then* you can be happy."

Her crescendo ended in a loud "It's bullshit!"

They both looked at Xander, who was doing his best to ignore them. Rebecca sipped her wine and said nothing. Tracy felt calmer after venting and was able to speak calmly once again.

"We are fine. We have food, clothes, a car that works, and a nice place to live. We are fine… and I will not abandon my son into the system."

"So, what's the difference?" Rebecca asked.

"What do you mean?"

"I mean what's the difference between him doing all of those normal things and what you're planning on doing with him... which is what, teaching him how to be poor?"

Tracy was done defending herself and spoke with confidence. "The difference is, he will learn how to be happy now and not believe he needs all of those other life-consuming things."

Xander smiled and silently thanked his mother. Even though she never had such a direct discussion about the system with him, her example and his witnessing this and other conversations taught him well that happiness now is more valuable than all the money and education in the world.

Now, he thought, *how can I pass that knowledge on to Paul?*

CHAPTER 44

X ANDER tried not to let Paul's situation affect him. He knew it would only if he allowed it to. Still, he wanted to figure out a way to help his friend realize that he didn't have to settle, that it was worth making choices that make him happy. Without letting it monopolize his time, he brainstormed and was thinking about talking with Paul as he went to check the mail. He used his key to open the small door and pulled out a single envelope with no return address. His felt his heart pound as he looked at the handwriting and recognized it as Serenity's.

He hurried back into his apartment with the envelope and sat down in his chair by the window to read it. Emotions and memories of their last kiss rushed through him as he stared at the envelope, but he had learned enough to know it would be best for him to detach from any expectations before exploring the contents. He placed the enveloped down on the window sill and went into the kitchen to make a cup of tea, figuring the physical separation from the letter could only help. He recharged his energy while his tea steeped, and he meditated to ensure he was deeply rooted in a place of self-love. Then he carried his tea back to the window sill and sat down.

He used his thumb to open the envelope and then slid a forefinger along the top, ripping an opening wide enough to retrieve the contents. He pulled out a small stack of lined paper folded in thirds. He unfolded them to reveal a three-page, handwritten letter and a small photo. He picked up the photo with one hand and stared at a vertical strip of four head shots of Serenity. It was cut unevenly and appeared to be a strip like the ones from a booth in the mall. She did not look posed, but like she just looked at the camera and snapped four quick pictures. Her hair was down around her shoulders, and she had most of a smile. To Xander, that was perfect. He reached out and imagined he could feel the comfort of her true blue energy cloud.

He set the pictures down, sat back, and read the letter.

Hi, Xander.

As you probably figured out by now, I moved and changed my number. It wasn't because of you, mind you, I just wanted a change. Since I didn't include my return address, I guess I am still figuring out what I want. Obviously, I am still thinking about you and I want to share a couple of things I wasn't ready to share before.

First, about my behavior the last time we spoke... I don't believe in apologies, so I hope you're not expecting one. If I had done something on accident, then it was just that, an accident, and if I had done something on purpose, then an apology doesn't make sense. Anyway, we know we're responsible for our own feelings. Having said that, I do want to explain my behavior.

I told you it was not a good thing to interfere with someone's aura, what you call energy cloud, without asking the person and without the person wanting you to do it. The reason is I used to do it all the time and, on one occasion, it backfired... big time, and it's the one thing I've done in my life that I still haven't managed to emotionally detach from in a healthy way. It came up so suddenly last time, I just didn't feel ready to talk about it at the time. To use your words, I hadn't "charged my energy" first. Well, I have now, so here it goes.

I've been able to see, feel, and use my energy for as long as I can remember. I'm not sure whether I was born with it or if I just learned it early, like you, but I quickly figured out I could do the same with other people's energy as well. I learned that I could use my own energy to influence and even control their energy, but I thought it was okay, because I always had good intentions when I did it. I became really good at it and, before you know it, I could adjust the energy anywhere I was to make things better. If people were in bad moods, I would make them happy. If people were sick, I would heal them or help them heal, unless it was really bad. I never told anybody about what I could see or what I could do. I guess that's because, in my experience, people don't believe what they can't see, and when they can see, they're afraid. In hindsight, I should have at least tried.

Anyway, like I said, I was really good at it. When I was ten, I overheard my parents talking. My mom was telling my dad that she was thinking about divorce. She said it was nothing he had done, that she had just changed. Her confession didn't surprise me too much. For some reason, she was never very maternal. I think her mom was the same way, so that makes a little sense. The bottom line is we never had the same bond that I've seen with other moms and their kids. It was okay, because my dad's paternal instinct made up for my mom's lack.

My dad was upset at my mom's decision, but he said he understood. Somehow, he talked her into staying until I was older, and she agreed to stay at least until I was out of elementary school. I was shocked at my mom's decision, but more disappointed. I wasn't disappointed in my mom, but in myself. I had not seen or felt anything unusual in my mother's aura, so there was nothing I could fix.

My mom stayed at the house, but in a different bedroom than my dad. He did his best to be positive about the situation, but I could see he was really sad most of the time. I was constantly manipulating his aura to make him feel better, but it never lasted long. After a while, I grew tired and started feeling a little depressed myself, so I stopped checking his aura, figuring that he would eventually get over the hurt. I didn't even notice when he got sick.

He was diagnosed with prostate cancer about six months after my mom had made her declaration. As soon as he got sick, though, her whole attitude seemed to change. She returned to the doting and attentive wife she used to be. She even moved back into the bedroom with him to take better care of him. She was completely sincere, and despite my dad being sick, he was truly happy again. I thought I could help him get better and he would be happy again.

We could be happy again. So I worked with his energy and helped him heal himself. No one knew what was happening, they only thought it was a miracle that his cancer completely disappeared in a matter of a few weeks.

Apparently, my mom felt guilty when my dad got sick, and after I healed him, she decided she didn't want to take a chance on being stuck in a life she didn't want. She left us a week later, and we haven't heard from her since. I understood that and I didn't take it personally. I know she loved us, just not enough to be a family. My dad may have healed from the cancer, but he hasn't been truly happy since, and no amount of energy work I have been able to do has been able to keep him happy. Had I not interfered, my father may or may not have been cured, but he may have eventually gotten over my mom and been able to be happy again.

We each choose what we do, what we think, how we feel, but we can only choose for ourselves because, regardless of our intentions, we can't know the outcomes of our actions.

That's why I left. I said I needed a change, but I didn't trust myself not to interfere with your life to get what I want... you. We're more alike than you know. I believe you and I are more aware of some things in life than most other people. Not better, just evolved to be able to see things differently. We don't lie to ourselves, and we can see that happiness and self-love are the most important things in the world, not society's expectations. Anyway, I know you have been learning to love yourself and I didn't want my desire to be with you to change your priorities. I knew if I told you that you'd say I can't control you and you're right, but I can control me, and that's what I'm doing.

I love you, Xander. I don't need you, but I want you, and I would choose you if we were together. I just want us both to be ready for that if it ever happens. And if it's meant to happen, I believe it will.

Xander blinked so he could see through the tears that had pooled in his eyes. The letter was signed, *Living in the now, but hoping for the future, Serenity.*

He reread the letter, wiped his eyes, and then threw the letter in the trash. He would remember the last part and would not need to read it again. She loved him. He didn't need to know that to be happy, but he was also happy he did. He would probably never forget it or her, but he would go on with his life in the same way Serenity was—living in the now, but hoping for the future.

CHAPTER 45

THE more Xander continued to practice his healthy selfishness, his own term for self-love, the easier it was to do and the happier he became. As his insecurities and other fears diminished, he found that vigilance in his practices was necessary. He still felt emotions and, at times when he was caught off guard, he would react based on the emotions. The more he practiced, the quicker he remembered to bring his awareness back to the present and focus on the here and now. That usually did the trick, since any negative emotions were usually based on something that had just happened or were a momentary worry about the future.

A few weeks had passed since he had last talked to Paul, and he wondered how his friend was doing. Although Xander wanted to help his friend and thought that he would be able to convince him that he was making some unhealthy choices, he had refrained from doing so after realizing that his own ego had commandeered his thinking on the subject and that he was judging Paul's actions. He also remembered what Serenity had told him about interfering, and his subsequent decision not to do so unless it was an emergency. Xander knew that Paul's life choices were part of his personal growth, and neither getting a girlfriend nor a starting new job classified as an emergency.

Still, he wondered how his friend was doing. So he texted him to see when they could meet to catch up. They spoke a couple of times over the course of a week, but they never found a mutually convenient time to meet. Paul always seemed to be busy with work or with Allison. Xander said he understood, but Paul sounded tense whenever they talked, and Xander had a feeling that financial troubles may be another reason Paul chose not to meet with him. His feeling was validated the next time they spoke.

The store where Xander worked had a bulletin board at the front where patrons could post general announcements and notices, which he would occasionally peruse. He was looking at it one day while on his break, and his attention was drawn to a brightly colored flyer. After reading it, he grinned, snapped a picture of it with his phone, and decided to call Paul after work.

After finishing a salad for dinner, he straightened up the kitchen and sat down in his chair by the window. He called up the photo of the flyer and then called Paul.

"Hey, Xander," Paul answered.

Xander thought he sounded preoccupied and didn't want to talk. "Hey, Paul. So, there's a line-up of guitarists playing at the park tomorrow night, and they're roping off the area and serving beer, wine, and appetizers. You in?"

"That sounds awesome, X-man, but I don't know."

"Oh… are you working or do you have plans with Allison?"

"No, but…"

"Did I mention it's my treat?"

Xander heard Paul inhale and then exhale as a sigh. "Well…"

Xander didn't let him finish. "I'll pick you up at seven."

"Okay. Thanks, man."

"No problem, Paul. See you tomorrow."

Xander arrived at Paul's apartment a few minutes early, but Paul was ready and they left right away. They made small talk on the short drive to the park, with both asking the other how work was going and Xander asking how things were going with Allison. According to Paul, they were going well.

They had to park a block from the event, but the temperature had started to cool and they enjoyed the short walk. They joined the line to buy tickets and enter the park when Paul put a hand on Xander's shoulder.

"Thanks for this."

Xander was surprised, and one look into Paul's eyes told him it was more than a casual thank you.

"Anytime, Paul."

They entered the park and lined up again in the concessions line, where Xander bought them both beers and a cardboard bowl of nachos to share, and then they found a table as close to the center of the audience and the speakers as they could, with hopes of maximizing the sound quality of the music. The agenda contained nine guitarists playing various songs, with a break after every three performances. Both Xander and Paul were enjoying the show and the refreshments, but just as the second intermission started, Xander looked at Paul and saw that he was already tired. He glanced at his energy cloud and saw a vibration within it associated with stress.

"You okay?" he asked.

Paul shook his head and blinked several times. "Yeah. Just tired. You know... work and stuff."

Xander felt torn between letting it go and having Paul clarify what he meant by "stuff." The two beers were enough to tip the scale to the latter.

"How are you doing, Paul?"

"No, really... I'm just tired."

"No, Paul, how are you doing?"

If Xander had expected a bit more resistance, he would have been disappointed. Paul dropped his head into his hands and then lifted his head and slid his hands over his hair and down to the back of his neck.

"Dude, I'm losing it."

Xander took advantage of the opportunity to delve even further. "What do you mean?"

"I'm working all the time, but I can't seem to get ahead. Whenever I'm off and not completely exhausted, Allison's either working or studying, and when we do have time together, we usually just have a cheap carry-out dinner and end up watching a movie or playing a game."

"Okay, so you're both busy. What's the problem?"

Paul's hands slapped the table in front of him.

"My life is boring, that's the problem! Why would she want to be with me when she could have so much better? I mean, she works with doctors. Guys who can afford to treat her like she deserves to be treated."

Xander knew that between the beers and Paul's lack of self-love that he probably wouldn't be open to hearing the truth—that he was sacrificing his actual happiness for what he thought was happiness.

"How do you know she wants that?"

Paul cocked his head to one side and looked confused, so Xander elaborated. "How do you know she wants to be with a doctor? Why do you think she cares about money? Has she told you that?"

"Well, no, but..." Paul began.

"And what makes you think you don't deserve her?"

Paul looked puzzled for a moment, but then he shook his head to dismiss Xander's words. "That's easy for you to say. You're living off a million-dollar inheritance. You could get any girl you want."

Xander grinned and took the last swallow of his beer. "I haven't touched my inheritance."

Paul pulled his head back in surprise. "You're shitting me."

"I'm not. I haven't touched a penny of it. You've seen where I live. I'm living off what I make at the store."

Paul still wore his look of surprise. "But why?"

Xander thought about the question. *Why don't I use my inheritance?*, he thought. *Because I don't need it to be happy.*

"I like to live simply. I've learned that the less I want, the happier I am." He tilted his head in thought and then nodded at the truth of his words.

Paul just stared at him. Eventually he spoke up. "Whatever. I just need more. I want more. And I don't want to lose her."

That's the problem, Xander thought. *You think you need her.*

"Paul... everyone, including you, deserves to be happy. That means if you are unhappy with yourself at any time, even being with someone... including Allison... then you deserve better."

Paul was clearly defensive now, but even he didn't know why. "I am happy... when I'm with her. She's awesome to me."

"So why don't you feel awesome when you're not with her?"

The last set started, and they watched it without speaking. Xander didn't argue when Paul again said he was tired, so they left as soon as it finished. They talked about the show on the short drive to Paul's apartment, and Paul thanked him as he got out of the car. Paul started to turn away, but Xander called to him.

"Hey, Paul. Allison sounds terrific... and I'm happy if you're happy. Seriously. It's just..."

"It's just what?" Paul snapped.

"It's just… when you met, she obviously liked you because of who you were and how you were living."

"So?"

"So, it just doesn't make sense that she would ask you to change for her."

"She didn't ask me to change."

Xander could see that Paul was thinking about his own words. He knew he could ask Paul why he was changing if she hadn't asked and point out the changes that Paul had already made, but he also knew that arguing would only push Paul away and stop him from listening.

"That's good."

"See you," Paul said, nodding, and continued to his apartment.

Xander drove away, hoping Paul would not lose himself trying to make someone else happy, but also reminding himself that whatever Paul chose was what he needed to experience.

CHAPTER

A CALL from the insurance agent who had been involved with the receipt of his inheritance brought him downtown to sign a tax document that had been missed during the original processing. The office was on the twenty-sixth floor of one of the tallest and oldest buildings in the city. Xander could see and sense that the strange squealing and clunking noises made by the elevator made some of its passengers uneasy as they ascended. As the individual people reached their chosen stops, Xander thought they seemed anxious to exit the car. He even heard one lady sigh as she stepped out, as if she had been holding her breath.

He was in and out of the office in less than five minutes, and when the elevator doors opened for him, he stepped into the car which was already carrying a dozen or so other people. Xander automatically noticed the diversity of the group, with several people in sharp business attire, some women wearing the latest trendy casual style, a young mother making faces and baby talk at the infant in a stroller, and teens huddled together while watching something funny on one of their smartphones. There was also a tall, lanky man with an overgrown beard, wearing cargo shorts, a tank top, and flip-flops. The man reminded Xander of Paul, and he grinned at the thought of his friend.

Xander could sense their energy clouds, but nothing stood out enough to get his attention, so he ignored them and began practicing his meditation, where he focused on his empirical senses one by one. The elevator ran smoothly down for the first couple of floors, but then two loud clunks and a flicker of the lights took all the passengers by surprise. Xander felt sudden tension in the energy clouds surrounding him and assumed it was noticeable to him only because they had all changed at once. The car continued to descend, and the passengers each reacted to the startling noises in their own way. One of the businesspeople joked about it, and his companions laughed and a couple of other passengers chuckled. The young mother was reassuring her baby, though the baby either had not noticed the strange sounds or had already forgotten them. In fact, all of the passengers seemed to have moved on to new thoughts, which is why the next thing that happened shocked them all.

Several of the passengers, including Xander, were watching the illuminated floor indicator light move through the long row of numbers. At least, Xander appeared to be watching them, but was more focused on his meditation. Just as the indicator light lit up the number fifteen, a loud screech was heard, the lights went out, and the elevator tilted off-balance, slowed, and stopped. Several people screamed as the tilted car caused everyone to slam against others as they fell to one side.

At first, it was sheer panic from most of the people. The ones against the wall tried to push the others off them, and the ones leaning on others tried their best to stand and scoot uphill toward the other side. A small emergency light came on, and that helped decrease the chaos. Those who fell were able to stand or at least use the small rail to pull themselves over so they weren't putting their weight onto others.

Xander was bombarded by the energy shifts of the others and was affected more by that than he was physically. He bruised his shoulder when it hit the corner of the door frame, but he managed to stop himself from crashing into one of the businessmen. Even in the dim light, it was clear nobody had sustained any serious injuries, though the tall, lanky man that reminded Xander of Paul was rubbing a large bump on his forehead. The young mother was crying, but the stroller had remained upright, and the blankets padding the sides of the stroller had protected the baby.

The car vibrated and dropped a couple of inches, causing more screams. Two of the businessmen had scrambled to the doors and were trying to pry them open with their hands. The tall, lanky man helped, but the angle of the car made it too difficult, and they were unable to budge them. Just then, a voice crackled through a speaker near the door.

"The fire department is trying to lock the car so it can't drop any further. As soon as they do that, they'll work on getting the doors open. Please remain calm and we'll have you out of there as soon as possible."

Xander could see and feel the energy associated with fear growing and gaining strength in the clouds around him, and in his own. He felt momentarily lost, but the screams from another short drop snapped him out of it and he was able to recognize the futility of his own fear and decided to charge his energy to calm himself.

He pictured light green energy running up from the ground far below him and filling him up, while pure, bright white energy surged into him from all around. He felt better immediately and, since there was nothing he could do but wait, he continued to charge his cloud, allowing the energies to expand.

He stood leaning into a corner with his energy expanding, sensing the fear in the people around him and wishing he could do something to calm them, but not knowing how. So the happy accident that occurred next came as a complete surprise to him. Although he did not direct it or even intend it to happen, as the energy he was using to charge his own cloud expanded, it came in contact with the clouds of the others in the elevator. The effect of the energy seeping into their clouds had the same calming effect on them as it did on Xander.

Of course, Xander thought as he remembered that all energy was connected and realized that what he thought of as charging was tapping into the unlimited energy source provided by the universe. He breathed deeply and felt the energy flowing through his body to the other clouds and through them and back out into space, only to return to him. The people were all but silent when the end of a crowbar appeared between the elevator doors.

Once the doors were opened, emergency responders helped everyone climb out and treated the minor injuries. After examining Xander and taking his contact information, they released him and he left the building by the stairs.

CHAPTER

XANDER was happy. He read, took walks, meditated, watched people from his living room window, and thoroughly enjoyed his new job as an assistant to the caretaker at the local botanical gardens. He had still been working at the grocery store and hadn't been looking for a new job, but he jumped at the opportunity for outside work. He had signed up for a couple of free courses offered at the community center, including a gardening class taught by a staff member at the gardens. Never having tried his hand at gardening before, he was surprised by how much he enjoyed the feel of his hands in the soil. The instructor, a master gardener who introduced himself as Pete, was impressed by Xander's sincere interest and his many questions. He encouraged Xander to apply for a newly opened position at the gardens and said he would put in a good word for him with the executive director.

Xander was hired two weeks later and at a modestly higher wage than he had been earning at the store. He loved working outdoors in the sun, and even in the occasional light rain. The work was sometimes physically challenging, but it was not complex. It allowed him to observe the energy clouds of the plants and many visitors the gardens hosted on a daily basis and to meditate while walking through the garden on his breaks. Also, he and Pete had become friends, an added benefit of which was that Pete taught him about the nutritional value of many herbs, fruits, and vegetables. Xander took advantage of his new friend's knowledge to improve his own eating habits and overall health.

The job was nearly full-time, and he was able to save money and travel by bus on the weekends to other cities and the adjacent states. His pleasures were simple and inexpensive, and his life was simple, and he was loving it.

One day after work, he wanted a smoothie and decided to buy one at the shop where Paul worked. It had been a few weeks since the concert, and they hadn't spoken since Xander had dropped him off. He didn't know whether Paul would be working, but even if he wasn't, Xander would be able to enjoy a smoothie and think about where he wanted to explore on his next bus ride.

He walked into the shop but didn't see Paul behind the counter. After a second of disappointment, he ordered his drink and was waiting for it at the pick-up counter when he heard his nickname.

"X-man!" Paul said. He had just emerged from the back wearing a huge, toothy grin.

He's glowing, thought Xander. He was amazed by the obvious positive change that had come over Paul since the last time he had seen him. Paul's energy and mood were the brightest Xander had ever seen from him.

"Hey, Paul. Wow… you look great. Did you win the lottery or something?"

"Do you think I'd still be working here? No lottery, but things are awesome!"

Paul's giddiness was contagious, and Xander couldn't keep from smiling.

"Can you join me for a few? I just ordered a smoothie."

"No can do. I just got off my break… but how about tonight? Want to grab a beer or something?" He paused and then added, "You may have to buy."

Xander laughed. Paul seemed like his old self, but even happier.

"Why don't you come to my place? I have some beer in the fridge, and I'll make us dinner."

"Sweet! Is five o'clock too early? I'm starving."

Xander laughed again. "See you then."

He picked up his smoothie and decided to head home via the store to pick up something simple for dinner.

Paul showed up almost thirty minutes early, but Xander didn't mind. They made small talk over a beer, and then Xander started making stir fry and rice for their dinner. Paul was surprised when Xander mentioned his new job, and he seemed genuinely interested in hearing about it. Eventually, Xander asked about Allison and how they were doing together.

"Awesome, man! After... well, after we talked, I thought a lot about what you said. You were right... I forgot that I actually like myself, so I talked to Allison. I told her that I really liked her, but that I like myself, too, and that I didn't care about making a lot of money, that I don't mind walking and taking the bus, and blah, blah, blah, yada, yada, yada."

Xander grinned at Paul's excitement and at the fact that he seemed truly happy with his life, but more importantly, with himself.

"So, what did she say?" he asked.

"That's the best part! She said she didn't want me to change... that she likes me because I was..." He paused, trying to remember. "... unreasonably happy with life! You were right all along, X-man... she likes me for the happy slacker that I am!"

"She sounds like a keeper. That's fantastic, Paul. I'm so happy for you... for you both."

"Thanks. You know what would make me happier? If we could eat... like now!"

Xander laughed. He was just finishing up the stir fry and dished them each plates with rice covered with a lot of vegetables and a little bit of marinated chicken. They ate and talked and laughed over dinner, and then watched a comedy movie and laughed some more. After the movie, Paul stood up to go.

"Want a ride?" Xander asked him.

"Oh, sure... you offer me a ride when it's nice and cool out, but not when I'm melting and sticking to the asphalt," he joked, referring to the day they met. Xander got the joke and chuckled.

"With as much dinner as you ate, I just wasn't sure those skinny legs of yours could carry the weight."

"I can eat a lot more rabbit food than that, X-man."

Xander stood up, walked him to the door, and reached out to shake his hand. Paul accepted his hand but pulled him into a quick hug.

"Thanks, man... for everything." He turned and walked down the steps.

"Take care, Paul. Say hi to Allison for me. I can't wait to meet her and tell her the real truth about you."

Paul smiled and nodded at him and headed down the walk. Xander watched him for a few seconds, admiring the peaceful-looking energy cloud that enveloped him.

CHAPTER 48

THE more Xander watched people and looked at the world around him, the more he understood how important it was to love himself and to choose to be happy. And he found that the more he loved himself, the less room and reason there was for insecurities, fear, or worry. If he did happen to experience one of those unhealthy feelings, his meditation, positive affirmations, and other self-love practices allowed him to quickly realize it, and he would remind himself that he was inherently connected to everyone and everything in the universe, and so there was nothing to judge.

He continued to watch people and their energy clouds wherever he went, and it was clear to him that one understanding—the interconnectedness of the energy in the universe—is what prevents self-love and happiness for so many. He believed that, in general, people were taught from childhood how and what to think. Parents, education systems, governments, and mainstream society prioritized life, but self-love was not among those priorities. He had watched people his whole life and noticed that most seemed to feel that they needed to be doing something with their lives to be happy. His mother had thought differently than many parents, so she didn't teach Xander that college, career, and retirement were necessary, sequential steps to happiness. He never learned that a person needed to be productive to be happy, but that a person could choose to be happy without having to do something with their life. A person could be happy simply by being.

He wondered why that understanding wasn't clear to most people and wanted to share his knowledge with others. He assumed that his interest in energy stemmed from his being able to see energy clouds, and figured that would explain the disparity. He meditated on finding a way to pass along what he had realized, and the answer came to him late one night as he was writing about it in his journal. He would write a book—a book about his epiphanies and the experiences that led to his relatively unique understanding of people and the world. And he would be happy doing it because it was not something he had to do, but something he wanted to do. He wondered what people would think of what he had to say, and then he was again thankful for his self-love practices and reminded himself that what other people think doesn't change anything. *The people who are ready to see the truth will be the ones who read it and believe it*, he told himself.

He didn't make notes and he didn't plan it out. He would write it when he was ready to write it, and it would take as long as it takes. There was no need to rush, no need to choose to feel like he had to be productive with it, which would be doing the very thing he was warning people not to do. He would write when he felt like writing.

What he felt like doing lately was reading, and his interest in quantum physics had recently been renewed. He was especially fascinated by what he had read about how observation affects reality and how expectations can determine what manifests in the reality that surrounds each of us. Xander understood that to mean experiences and events in life happen based on how we see the world... how we chose to see the world. When he extrapolated his understanding of that principle, he knew that only things a person believed could manifest in their lives.

With that thought, he decided to conduct an experiment. He would try to change his thinking so that his beliefs were not limited to what he had personally experienced or knew that someone else had experienced. He would try to be open to anything.

He remembered a comment Paul had made about how he, Xander, was able to find a front parking spot whenever he wanted, and he wondered whether that was the result of him simply believing it was possible and that it would happen. Thinking it not only plausible, but probable, he decided he would try to re-create the results as opportunities presented themselves.

He soon realized he would not have to wait long for those opportunities, they were everywhere.

Finding an available front parking space was only one small example. He obtained similar results with other things. When he was shopping and the store happened to be out of one of his favorite products, he would just happen to find a stray one in a completely different section. He wanted to buy a single, organic granola bar that he always enjoyed, but the box in the produce section was empty. Rather than settle for one he didn't enjoy as much, he focused on his intention to find one of the ones he liked. He only had a few items, but the self-checkout line was crowded, so he jumped in line in a nearly empty regular line. When it was his turn to pay, he noticed three of his favorite granola bars next to the register. A previous customer had changed his mind about buying them, and they had not yet been restocked.

"What a coincidence," Xander told the cashier. "That's just the kind I was looking for."

"Lucky you," replied the cashier.

"Lucky me," replied Xander, although he didn't believe it was luck.

Another successful demonstration in Xander's mind was on a night he and Paul had agreed to go to the movies. The showing was in the early evening on a day Paul was working, so Xander was picking him up from work, and they would go straight to the theater. Xander was on time, but an unexpected crowd at the smoothie bar kept Paul busy. When his supervisor finally let him leave fifteen minutes late, Paul moped out from around the counter to where Xander was waiting.

"Sorry, man. I guess we'll have to try it another time."

Xander looked at his phone for the time. "Maybe it's not too late. Let's try to make it."

Paul looked at his own phone. "No way. Even with the previews, we'll miss the beginning... and that's if we don't buy any popcorn."

"Let's try anyway. What do we have to lose? Worst thing that happens is we miss it and then we do something else. Come on."

Xander turned and headed for the door, and Paul sighed and followed.

They reached the box office ten minutes after the advertised start time, but Xander approached the window as if nothing was wrong.

"Two for the seven o'clock showing, please."

"You're lucky," said the young girl behind the glass. "Someone hit a transformer earlier and our power was down for a few. It's back up now, so we're running a bit behind. The previews should just be starting."

Xander smiled. "Yeah, lucky." He took the tickets and thanked the girl.

Since it was late, there were no lines at the concession stands, and they were able to buy popcorn and drinks and find seats just as the movie was starting.

Xander smiled again and glanced at Paul, who was staring at him and shaking his head.

"Man, you are one lucky dude."

There's that word lucky again, he thought.

It didn't always work, but Xander realized he was never any worse off when it didn't. It was all a matter of how he chose to look at the situation.

The secret is to know what I'd like to happen, believe that it will happen, but don't worry about how it happens, and detach from the outcome so I'm not disappointed if it doesn't happen, he told himself.

He knew that things that happened also had to do with the one universal energy that made up everything. He just wasn't sure how it worked, and he knew better than to worry about it. What was important is that he had proven to himself that the energy of his intentions and how he chose to look at life had a direct impact on what and how things happened in his life.

Another thing to write about in my book, he thought, *if and when I write it. No*, he corrected himself, *if I want it to happen… it will.*

CHAPTER 49

ONE warm, sunny day, Xander was working at the botanical gardens removing leaves from some flower beds that had been planted below a large tree. It was a slow and tedious process because he had to remove each leaf by hand so as not to hurt the flowers with a rake or other gardening tool. He was kneeling, supporting his upper body weight with one hand and picking leaves with the other. Once his hand was full, he would give himself a small shove backward until his balance carried him into a sitting position. He had just dumped a handful of dried leaves into his mulch bag when a strange, familiar feeling came over him, a warm and comforting feeling that gave him the slightest tickle in his stomach. He wiped the sweat from his brow with his forearm and looked back over his shoulder to one side and then the other. He saw Serenity walking toward him.

Xander stood up and dusted himself off, and then looked into the most beautiful eyes he had ever seen.

"Hey," he said, surprised.

"Hey, yourself," she answered, pulling him into a hug, which he happily returned.

"I'm all sweaty."

"Yes, I can see that… and smell it," she said, chuckling.

"What are you doing here?" Xander asked.

"Looking for you. Your friends at the grocery store told me of your betrayal and where I could find you."

Xander smiled. He missed her wit and everything else about her, but it was different now. He was okay without her, too.

"Yeah, they weren't all too happy when I left. Anyway, it looks like you found me. What are you doing back?"

"I felt like taking a semester off. Of course, my counselor strongly advised against it. She said most students who take a semester off never finish."

"What did you say to her?" asked Xander.

"I told her I'm not most people and I don't care what they do."

"I'll bet she loved that."

"Yeah. She's probably already archived my file."

Xander just looked at Serenity and appreciated her. He no longer felt he needed her, but he loved her just the same.

"You look different," she said to him. "Like you have a secret."

Xander just kept smiling and loving her. "I have a couple more hours here. Would you like to get together later and catch up?"

"Sure. Just give me a call when you're done working. Here's my number," she said, handing him a slip of paper.

She tilted her head and looked like she was trying to read his mind. After a couple of seconds, she seemed to relax and returned his loving look.

"It's good to see you, Xander."

"It's good to see you, too, Serenity."

She turned and left, and Xander watched her until she was out of sight.

After he left work, he went home and showered and then sent Serenity a text to arrange a rendezvous. She said she had already eaten dinner, so they agreed to meet for a drink at a local café with an outside seating area to enjoy the cool evening weather.

They both dressed casually, and there was no awkwardness whatsoever. Serenity told Xander all about her college experiences, her new friends, and the latest books and movies she enjoyed. Afterward, she asked all about his life since they had last spoken, and he told her everything he could remember. He found himself getting excited when he was telling her about his idea for a book and was pleased that she seemed excited, too.

"It would be pretty cool to be able to… to help other people see what we see," he told her.

"Why? Is how we see things better than how others see them?" she asked, eyeing him suspiciously.

Xander knew Serenity was not trying to argue with him, but even if she had been, he felt no need to become defensive.

"Not at all. It's just a different perspective, and I think it would be nice for people to know what other options they have."

Serenity smiled and sipped her drink.

They talked for a couple of hours, with Serenity speaking to Xander more openly and easily than she ever had before. *Something has changed,* thought Xander. Serenity looked at her phone and called for the check.

"I got us this time," she said, looking at Xander.

"Thank you," was all he said.

"Wow. You really have changed."

She signed for the check and retrieved her small purse from the back of her chair, and then they walked to the street together. They stopped just outside the café entrance to say their goodbyes.

"So, what are you doing tomorrow?" Xander asked.

"No plans... although I may go to the park." She gave Xander a big hug. "See you soon."

"Good night," Xander said as he watched her walk away. *You may see me sooner than you think.*

EPILOGUE

THE next morning, Xander woke early and did nothing special. He meditated, exercised, and ate breakfast. Afterward, he showered, dressed, and read, and then headed to the park. Serenity did not say what time she would be going, and Xander had no idea if she would be there at all. He was just doing what he felt like doing, although he put out his intention that he would see her. In any case, it was a gorgeous day, and he would enjoy himself at the park.

He didn't rush to get there, and when he arrived, he casually strolled around the park like he usually did, looking, listening, and thinking. While crossing the one small bridge near the center of the park, he leaned over the side to watch some ducks, and he heard his name.

"Xander!"

He turned and saw Serenity. She approached and hugged him, then held him at arm's length, looking stern.

"Please don't tell me you're still chasing me."

"Not chasing you exactly, but I was hoping to find you."

Serenity sighed, shook her head and looked ready to say something, but Xander spoke first.

"But... I don't *need* you. This is just what I feel like doing now."

Serenity looked skeptical.

"Are you just saying that or do you really feel it?"

"I'm serious, Serenity. I love you. I do. But I love myself first."

She looked at him for several seconds and he noticed her glance at a spot just above his head. Then she looked directly into his eyes and smiled.

"Yes, you've changed." Then she wrapped her arms around his neck and kissed him long and deep. When they finished kissing, Serenity turned and took him by the hand and they started walking.

"Maybe later we could do something," she said to him.

"Maybe," he said in response.

"Or maybe later... we can just be."

AFTERWORD

LIKE so many people, I have been experiencing what I can only describe as an awakening of consciousness. That awakening has accelerated over the past several years and is ongoing, as I'm sure it will continue to be for the remainder of my life. This book is a compilation of the key lessons I have come to understand from my awakening, so far.

I did not write this book as an autobiography, although I do share many of my perspectives with the characters, namely Xander and Serenity. Also like Xander, I understand I am human and, as such, am imperfect and need to constantly remind myself that I have a choice of how I think, speak, act, and even feel. It is a perpetual practice, but since I love myself, I will always strive to better myself. Of course, when I say "better myself," I am not talking about working toward, earning, accomplishing, or obtaining anything. I'm talking about feeling and being. Specifically, feeling good and being happy.

I wrote my nonfiction book, *Mastering Your Choices*, which parallels many of the themes presented in this book, during my working years. During that same period, I had learned and understood many of the lessons I wrote about in *A Human… Being*, but had not yet chosen to overcome the fear that kept me imprisoned in a world based on control and expectations. When I finally accepted the truth that I create all my fear, I was able to begin freeing myself. I quit working in the prime of my second successful career, not to *pursue* my passion, but to *do* my passion… and you're reading the proof.

For those of you still caught in that limbo of fear, spending more than half of your waking day doing what you have to do instead of what you want to do, I offer this simple message: whenever you're ready, choose to stop working for a life and start loving how you live. In the best-case scenario, you will be immensely and financially successful, and in the worst-case scenario, you will still be doing what you love.

Most importantly, remember that you don't always have to be doing something to be happy. You don't have to wait until you've met any goals, until you're financially secure, or until you retire. Happiness is a choice, a state of being, and you can choose to be happy right now.

CPSIA information can be obtained
at www.ICGtesting.com
Printed in the USA
LVHW040516190723
752762LV00001B/10